Advance Praise for

The Long Swim

"Whenever I want to remember the pleasures and the possibilities of language, I read Terese Svoboda. I am awestruck by what she can make live out of flat language on paper—loose lions, knife-wielding children, black hole men and vibrant nude women, adulterers and newlyweds and orphans, the legless dog joyfully buoyant on life's 'long swim,' the unspeakable griefs and joys that curtain our lives like 'the pell-mell greeny rain.' This new collection is a lightning storm, revelatory and galvanic—I love *The Long Swim*, and Svoboda's crackling, hilarious, gorgeous prose-music."

—Karen Russell, author of *Orange World and Other Stories* and *Swamplandia!*

"These stories, so precise and joyful in language and movement, don't hesitate to dive meaningfully into heaviness and honesty. What musical and beautifully-written pieces to read aloud and savor."

—Aimee Bender, author of *The Particular Sadness of Lemon Cake*

"[This] collection is wry, often hilarious, and just as often sad, sad, sad. What a book! I admired the big and small surprises with each new gemlike tale. This is [a] confident collection that cultivates and builds on its own idiosyncrasy of vision. It makes a big promise and fulfills it entirely."

—Robin McLean, author of *Pity the Beast*

"Terese Svoboda is a master of the dire and the blackly comic and a virtuoso of economy and voice, and *The Long Swim* features the jaunty and the wounded who in extremis maintain their wit and lacerating self-awareness. These survivors apparently believe that all trouble should be loud and bold, generating emotional histories that are like reports from a battlefield, but they nevertheless find their way, through their diminished toolbox for negotiating trauma, toward cooperation and mutual regard."

—Jim Shepard, author of *The Book of Aron* and *The World to Come*

The Long Swim

The Long Swim

TERESE SVOBODA

UNIVERSITY OF MASSACHUSETTS PRESS
Amherst and Boston

ISBN 978-1-62534-807-4 (paper)

Designed by Sally Nichols
Set in Freight Text Pro
Printed and bound Books International, Inc.

Cover design by adam b. bohannon
Cover art by Katherine Bradford, *Woman In Water*, 1999,
oil on canvas, 68 x 80 inches. From the collection of the artist,
© Katherine Bradford.

Library of Congress Cataloging-in-Publication Data

Names: Svoboda, Terese, author.
Title: The long swim / Terese Svoboda.
Other titles: Long swim (Compilation)
Description: Amherst : University of Massachusetts Press, 2024. | Series:
Juniper Prize for Fiction |
Identifiers: LCCN 2023046530 (print) | LCCN 2023046531 (ebook) | ISBN
9781625348074 (paperback) | ISBN 9781685750770 (ebook) | ISBN
9781685750787 (ebook)
Subjects: LCGFT: Short stories.
Classification: LCC PS3569.V6 L66 2024 (print) | LCC PS3569.V6 (ebook) |
DDC 813/.54—dc23/eng/20231013
LC record available at https://lccn.loc.gov/2023046530
LC ebook record available at https://lccn.loc.gov/2023046531

British Library Cataloguing-in-Publication Data
A catalog record for this book is available from the British Library.

For Eric who went to Hollywood

———————————

You look ridiculous if you dance.
You look ridiculous if you don't dance.
So you might as well dance.

—GERTRUDE STEIN

CONTENTS

The Long Swim

Swordfished in Nantucket

The veteran's head rests in his hands. Maybe he's reading. A newspaper lies on the table a glance away. His glasses remain folded, stem on stem, beside him. It's early for a headache, or very late.

Let's go to the lost graveyard today, says his brother, wearing pajamas of the demanding sort, two plaids. He's just broken the glass part of a coffeemaker, dismissing the breakage with Coffee schmoffee, who needs it, his Texas enthusiasm undampened by broken glass or coffee-lack or even big/little brother estrangement. Let's see if that graveyard's still lost from last year.

They are two of five siblings and ten cousins vacationing by turns in Nantucket with their ninety-four-year-old patriarch. My husband, a beloved-enough cousin, has secured us a turn. Fortunately I'm no coffee drinker. I open the fridge and take out a carton of orange juice. I say Yes, let's.

The vet went to war and took up ski rescue on his return, shot cannons to clear avalanches until his bad back suggested: Why not invent an app to find these avalanches faster? He is in app-land now, and perhaps that makes his head ache. The vet looks hung over, but he doesn't drink—a response to the ninety-four-year-old's martinis. When he raises his head, he has that where-am-I-now look that ex-drinkers or users have, that vets can't get rid of. Didn't the graveyard sink into the pond?

The Texan considers the question, stirring milk into hot water that has been exposed to coffee grounds. Second in age to the vet, he has more faithfully followed his father by becoming a lawyer;

hence he's all about the consideration of questions. The story is, he says to me, they filled in the pond for the gravesites. Only later did they find out how hard it was to keep people buried in a swamp.

We called it resurrection in Nam, says the vet, in a growl I associate more with bears than unshaven men. But he's friendly despite the head-in-hands stance, he smiles. You got a cigarette?

Who me? I gesture. He wouldn't know I've never, this is the first year we've been invited.

His brother gives him the silent out-of-here flick and a cigarette at the same time. In boots, the vet walks over a glass shard or two and lights up at the gas range, a gesture from another class. Or maybe region. He's long been out of Texas, a state not celebrated for skiing opportunities.

I drink OJ while the Texan sweeps up. My nipples, now that I think about it, press visibly against my nightie. I want to hunch and enunciate *Who me?* with at least a hint of brains, I want to impress the Texan, not to mention this vet. Being the oldest makes the vet an age regression of his patrician father, none too shabby in the looks department. Women have thrown themselves into snowbanks at the very thought of his rescue.

The patriarch likes to sing. He can hardly read, and wears a magnifying glass that's practically a telescope on his chest, readied for the *Times* in the morning when his now ninety-five-year-old eyes work best—so forget a movie after dinner, let's sing. All the verses of every song from the 40s, which his five children know well from long car trips, which every one of them, even the vet, gussy up with trills and octave changes and chords a fourth lower—this is the kind of singing that changes their faces from those of bored middle-aged worriers into smiling carefree siblings no matter how much is or is not drunk or remembered.

I mumble along. The family's gifts to my husband don't include the ability to carry a tune, and his becomes heavier and heavier in the forced march from his brain to his larynx to his lips. He joins in the smiling. All the girl cousins smile back, sad they didn't land him, all consanguinity aside. This afternoon he saved his brother's stepson's girlfriend from drowning by stripping to his shorts and righting her tub-sized sailboat where the surf caught it. She wouldn't have drowned but she'd surely have gotten wet and, in this early fall cold, caught a terrible chill, which is what my husband has now, unable to strip off those shorts in front of the girlfriend. Did his brother or the girl thank him? Yes and no. She sailed away with a wave and was then driven to the airport, but here his brother comes now, back from dropping her off, ready to sing for the rest of the evening, no tune or missing-words problem with him. He comes over with his hand out, and cheer. They shake, my husband still shaking.

We have to wait two summers to visit the graveyard but then the Texan's sister drives us right up to its picnic table. She has a penchant for bows in her hair, and restrains the slightest unruly strand with the swipe of a single-bowed comb. She's the one who delivers the important information on the ride over re: the health of her father, whose child worries whom, and where to go for beer. The graveyard scene, she says, by way of introduction.

Why may not that be the skull of a lawyer? says the Texan who has biked up behind us, there not being room in the car for everyone and the big picnic basket.

His sister is so gracious, she assumes we are all on the same page vis-à-vis Shakespeare. She says, That lawyer you destroyed two weeks ago? Was it for love or money?

The Texan belly-laughs and grabs his wife's bike so it doesn't tip in the soft grass of the graveyard swamp. Revenge, he says.

With love he's more perverse, says his wife, whose long beautiful legs seem to start just under her chin. She's already ladling chowder into soup-sized coffee mugs.

We laugh while staring at the green meadow whose slight depression is all that suggests its other use—no bones stick up.

My husband and the vet arrive and roll in the meadow to show us there's no poison ivy.

Ticks, ticks, scream his girl cousins.

The men are so brave, and they chase the women with whatever they find.

Personal omelets, the Coloradan says, his drawling of the "om" originating from his state rather than the Texan's, he's an in-law like me, not cousined, a son-in-law. He's holding ten plastic bags, each with a beaten egg inside, and he insists that we add onion or pepper or cheese or mushrooms to our bags, to taste, including the patriarch. We line up and select our handfuls. The Coloradan sacrificed the entire morning's golf game to chop and beat the contents that we must now dunk into boiling water for a prescribed four minutes while thinking up jokes about Texans. He starts: A Texan and myself sat in a blind all day and never saw a thing. Then at about sundown, a lone duck flew overhead, so high you could hardly see it. When it was right overhead, the Texan raised his shotgun and fired—the Coloradan takes aim at the ceiling—but the duck kept right on flying. The Texan said, the Coloradan continues, winking at his Texan in-laws, Son, yore witnessing a miracle. Thar flies a dead duck.

The eldest daughter ministrates, stays up all night. It's hard to sleep in the same room as her father. He breathes, then stops. She eats all night to keep herself up, to console herself, for pleasure. In the morning light, haggard, she tells her father how nice he looks, his white sneakers with the soles glued back on, his red pants, his Brooks Brothers shirt. She puckers up and gives him a kiss on his half-shaven cheek.

The now ninety-six-year-old patriarch travels to the end-of-summer ritual at the dump, and the whole family accompanies him. At eleven sharp, the gates open and townspeople empty huge plastic bags of clothing onto a table surrounded by other townspeople ready to claim every sweater. WASPs are loath to pass up anything some fool nouveau riche jettisons. Broken-looking appliances are muscled away before they're unwrapped, shoes with ruined heels snatched up. No fighting! says the sign. No staying longer than thirty minutes. Another wave of townspeople arrives. No tag-teaming. No leaving pets.

I love my new tie-dye skirt but when I walk across the room, it slides to my knees, the elastic shot. After I untangle myself, the second daughter scoops it up and wears it on her head. Waste not, want not, she says, all sprightly camaraderie.

In the spring, after the snowmelt, the vet tells us, I sometimes take environmentalists up the mountain to scout endangered species. Three of them in their late 70s and 80s this year, but in great shape. I'm rushing to keep up, I'm huffing and puffing, when they all fall to their knees at the same time. I think they're having simultaneous heart attacks but, no, they're intent on examining something rare, its yellow bud about an inch off the soil. I don't have my right specs on so I have to lean down to look and I don't lean as well as I used to, so I do what I always do to inspect something out of my eyesight but within reach, I pluck it.

Oh, groan the three scientists.

Then I do the only thing I can: I eat the little yellow bud.

Banging between rooms. So dark it's almost light, black at its best. Doorknobs tried and walls banged again. Muffled *Whats?*

The Coloradan drank so much the night before he thought the wall was the door and why wouldn't it open? He and the Texan agree: it was almost Texan, his determination. They are tending the flames of the barbecue, Texas TV, the flaming sunset of charcoal and grease, swordfish on a platter with tongs beside it, laughing about all that banging in the middle of the night.

There is more liquor.

Sitting straight as the chair he occupies, the ninety-seven-year-old patriarch is just inside the screen door and is talking about the World Federation, not the sci-fi version but the post-WWI assembly of all the prelates united against war of any kind. The pope coming to Texas last week reminded me, he says, his jamming the traffic for a whole day brought up one of the few times in my life when peace was thought to be possible. It's a subject he savors, he swirls the red wine in his glass as if peace could be swallowed. The women in the kitchen a few steps away prepare salad or bread or crackers heaped with pink chopped bits, intent on their gendered labors. They tip their drinks so the cubes don't click, and close the oven softly with mitts so as to hear the patriarch's eloquence on solving the world's problems or just to listen to his brain work. Their brains, that inheritance, work just as surreptitiously. During the lost-graveyard expedition now two years ago, the Texan's sister revealed that she ran the office of the governor for years, then an entire college. All I'd thought she could do was write shopping lists. Can he quote Woodrow Wilson? is what she's wondering now. Not from shaking hands with him, no, Wilson didn't say anything to him then, she says, but from a documentary he saw last week.

He quotes Pope Benedict, whom the president from long ago snubbed.

Okay, she says, awed like the rest of us. She hands me a cocktail and maneuvers me into his line of fire, saying, He likes younger women to drink with.

That's most of us, I say, when you're his age.

The vet wants to tell us about a scary out-of-the-body experience.

His ninety-eight-year-old father says age is a scary in-body experience.

We toast to that.

I was trapped under the snow, says the vet. From below I thought I could hear what I thought were search dogs sniffing around the crevasse, and I howled at them. It turned out to be a snowcat.

No more wine for him, shouts the Coloradan.

I always believed my body was a prison, says the Texan. I was right. In biology I learned it was made of cells.

The next year the Texan trips and discovers a brain tumor as a result of his visit to emergency. He Skypes in that year, with instructions on how to grill the swordfish. In a hoodie and cap that both read *Nantucket!* and with one hand around a grill fork, he proclaims that the mayo has to be 100 percent American and applied on both sides.

Only the empty mug he's waving in his other hand lets on that he
can't drink, that failures of the body keep him away—his, and his
wife's, who jumped fifty feet into the family quarry at a prenuptial
bash for his son who's marrying Brazilian oil money, and hit a rock
instead of water. Air-lifted out, she witnessed the ceremony with
what was left of her leg in traction, while across the hospital her
daughter, traumatized by a sudden divorce, her mother's screams,
and her father's impending death, fell into a seizure.
We slather on American mayo.

The Colorado son-in-law follows Matt Damon and his girl from
the grocery store down to the dock to the very end, where quite
a big boat is tied up. Matt Damon says a lot of people think he's
Matt Damon, but Yes, he says, you can take your picture with me.
Scrutinizing the result, we decide he is Matt Damon, he damn well
looks like Matt Damon, he's not the South African second mate he
pretends to be, he is in character.
    I'm in character too, says the Coloradan son-in-law, providing a
lopsided smile. We all agree but we're missing the Texan. The vet
refuses to come, he's so sad, he sends his love in an actual letter.

Speaking of traffic jams, says the ninety-nine-year-old patriarch, my
granddaughter was selling plastic flamingos for charity years ago,
flocks of them piercing the lawn of our office downtown. The president
stopped his what-do-you-call-it?—motorcade—and bought three of
them. That president. I've distrusted him ever since. One flamingo
would have been okay, maybe. What a flirt. But I will vote for his wife.
    His walker has a name and he calls it as if it will trot across the
room to him, wagging a mechanical tail. Fetched by me, it gives
him lean-room, it lets him quote FDR: "It is common sense to take
a method and try it. If it fails, admit it frankly and try another. But
above all, try something." The patriarch had polio in his youth—
longer than FDR—and has walked with a cane all his life, naming his
canes too, spreading around every semblance of life to both animate
and inanimate, gearing up for his hundredth.

I don't mention his age when I tell him he walks pretty good for a guy with polio.

Why, thank you, he says, holding the door for me.

Your daughter says you still go to the office. How many lawyers do you have working under you?

Half, he says, his buried eyes alive.

Loose Lion

They pitchforked Old Gray on account of him sleeping in the dark part of the barn.

I don't blame them. I would've thought it were a lion too, says the party-line operator.

News like that makes the telephone here worthwhile. I was over at the Tickles' last yesterday, the Tickle Tickles', not Avery's bunch, when I heard that the lion was loose. Mabel Tickle tried to hush the operator then, but it was no good, she screeched and screeched, like the lion was on her lap.

Creeping through the jungle like a golden track, boomalaya, boomalaya, boomalaya, boom.

I don't care for poetry but Vachel Lindsay has it beat.

The boom makes all the little kids scream to mercy.

Likely. They got a posse making noise in the cornfield now. They'll find the lion and make mincemeat out of him, you'll see.

Mmmmm, lion sandwiches. I'll bet you could make a good-looking lion purse with what's left over from a rug. You know the governor's going to want the rug.

I paid twenty-five cents to see that circus show and they went on without the lion. They didn't give us a penny back. I guess the tamer had better look for a new job.

He better look for his old one. Now who is it you all would like to call?

———

Maybe it actually is a maneater like what it says on the poster, is what the lion tamer is thinking. The little ladies who hardly even scream *Oh!* go to church to see lions curled up with lambs, they never had a pig as nice as pie turn on them and try to bite off their hands. But, no, the lion tamer's lion really was as nice as pie. The tamer whacks at the cornstalks with the gun barrel, trying to scare it out. It's still too light to see the fires inside the houses over which such nice pie might be cooking, the settlements being close to the fields because a man can't farm much farther than he can keep a mule going with the plough. Which is a blessing because it's not much farther than a person could call out *Lion!*

Over eight feet tall! is what he shouted when the lion stood on its legs in the show to dance with him, husband to wife. He said maybe the townspeople should play the show music to get the lion to stand up again and somebody volunteered to hitch up a mare to lug the gramophone over rather than walk the field with the rest of them. Coward, shouted the others. Why, it was only two shows ago, sticking his head inside the lion's mouth, that that the lion tamer'd seen that bad tooth, black and yellow, going green.

Aunt Flo's second boy, supposed to be home for supper, gets off the first shot. Hardly grazed him, but still something. Then Hanrahan's hat fills with holes—it was dangling from the end of his rifle, thank god. A right jittery bunch, most of them. Colonel Horst the worst, the Civil War on his shoulder, each of the leaves on the cornstalk like a flag to him if there's any wind at all. Always boastful, he claims he surprised the lion and shot it in the leg but nobody was there to see him do it.

The circus says they want the lion back alive. They hire horses so they can see over the tops of the corn, and bring in the aerialist's nets so as to flush the lion out into them. After a week they pack up and move on.

The tamer stays put, out of a job without an animal, and boards for the time being with some woman known as Aunt Flo. He says the other circus was getting too close to theirs in the revenue department and there is nothing like a loose lion for publicity. Good, Flo asks, or bad? Listen to me, he says, last year six circus trains got wrecked and the animals all ran off. Now how would six of them wreck? No other kind of train wrecks so easy as that. It's just part of the act. He says he would have switched to contortionist if he'd known about the racket, or trained up a horse. A loose lion!

A week after the first search is called off, a horse goes missing, and parts of another. I'm going to leave what's left out for bait, says the fuming owner. He lays it, finished bleeding, on a circle of hay. It's not so fresh but maybe the lion isn't so fussy.

Not far away lie two lovers, one of them so against the killing of the lion that she keeps the other away from "the hunt of your life," as advertised for two weeks in the local newspaper, keeps him away by the oldest means possible. These two lovers are not married except to other people so each spouse assumes the other's elsewhere. He growls at her, she mews. They have found McHenry's good for them, a farmhouse abandoned in a battle between heirs. Since he is one of the heirs, he can keep the battle going. No one from either side is allowed entrance until it's settled. She has her alibis and since she is still so young and so newlywed, she hardly has to use them, and since he's a man he has places to go, whereas his bride doesn't. He is beating his way back to his own homestead, tra-la.

The bait is took is the news of the week, says the operator.

The lion isn't that big sitting down. The lover steps closer. It's not like a snake is what he thinks, you want to put out your hand and call to it. He doesn't yell or they'll know where he is and why he is in the wrong place at the wrong time, but he doesn't turn his back to it and run, that is suicide. It's been shot in the leg, it doesn't move when it sees him, its eyes narrow. He stares, he thinks he's casting his power over it, that it is paralyzed by his might. He has been drinking a cordial or two with his lover.

The lion shakes its head and a halo of dust rises, then it limps off. He tells everybody it sat somewhere else.

The Summers' boy, out calling their good trained dog that is running in the dark, drops his torch too close to a hay bale and it catches. Volunteers take all night to put out the fire. After it's over they find big bones all burnt up. They say they saw the lion raise itself up and jump through the fire like into a circus hoop but that the fire jumped higher.

The tamer isn't so sure about the bones. Could be a big badger or a cow's, he says. Did you find teeth?

Nobody found teeth.

Does the lion eat underwear, since Mame lost two from the line? is the kind of question they pepper the tamer with. He doesn't tell them how the lion scared the bejeezus out of him, always had, nice or not. He never could figure out, he swears, how the lion got past the bars of its cage, must've been some voodoo. In fact he was drunk when the first alarm got out, then he closed the empty cage quick where he had forgotten the latch. Earlier, he had sung to the lion as he gave it its dinner, making it turn its head where he put down its food, a bit short that week. The revenues were down too since he'd been refusing to put his head inside on account of that rotting tooth. Did he put his head inside that last time? He did. He had to or lose his job. People would come back again and again to see his head inside that lion. Maybe he left that door open because he was finished even thinking about that lion's tooth.

He is swinging a hammer for Kolste on the days the Kolste boy has to help at the post office.

She married into the region, leaving Chicago and Papa behind as so many girls do. Church-held suppers, as innocent as that, where the new wives do the dishes while the new husbands dry: that's how the two lovers met, when it didn't seem that she would ever meet anyone ever again. To quell this loneliness of hers, her father had bought her a radio. Sometimes it picked up the Chicago Symphony that she sits and listens to without moving, or else dances with her broom to the melodies. It is hardly dance music, and she weeps. Not so anyone can see, not in the open but in the kitchen just after the broadcast when she is making her new husband coffee. Sometimes her husband does see and catches her by the arm and asks if the floor is that dirty.

A fellow-feeling sweeps the town on account of its fame for having a lion lost in its whereabouts: beers are raised in toasts to the town's bravery, a newborn is named Tiger despite it being a lion that is lost, and the women's auxiliary draws up a coat of arms with the lion as a sort of human.

He is dolling himself up for her again, even adding a pinch of that scented talcum the city boys wear, and he is putting on his best shoes—Off to church? asks his wife, bending over laundry she's been refusing to do unless he makes peace with her in the bedroom way, which he has, he's done his duty, as hard as it is with her so pregnant, he is taking the short cut to McHenry's about a mile out of the way of his stated destination, he is passing the slate fall and the ashy quarter section and the fence nobody yet fixed at the bottom because there's a washout so close, a kind of natural fence the way he looked at it, he is leaning hard into the front door where it is warped from no woman to see to it properly, he hears her moving in the back where they like to go and he stops, adjusts his wardrobe in anticipation, his face showing red in the ratty old mirror of the foyer, he pulls the inside door toward him.

She's in the corner in the half light of the old curtains rotted and torn, she's in the corner lying there with someone else.

No.

The man steps forward the way he didn't before. The lion rises, an arm falling to one side. Because of its hurt leg, it doesn't lunge, the man lunges, and the powerful stench of the lion's mouth and its paw knock him to the floor. Scrabbling up, he pulls at her body, which is not the thing to do.

Afterward, the lion jumps out the window they left open.

What is leftover of the woman her husband has a hole dug for and weeps beside her radio. How did that man who found her know where to look? And in his best clothes? The phone operator guesses why and says so. They don't put up much of a monument for him.

When a moose wanders into town the very next year, someone shoots it right off.

The tamer runs for sheriff. Vote for me, he says. I'll protect you. Nobody else wants the job, too dangerous, and having him stay on means that if the cat comes back, they can put him out as bait. What he does is take all that he saves from sheriffing and put it into stocks. Everybody else who has two cents to his name is doing that, never mind paying for a new planter. The Roaring Twenties may be just about over, but this time he's not going to be left behind, he'll roar too.

Rain People

The leather-jacketed crew of *Rain People* smoked pot, which we swore was alfalfa, it smelled so sweet. Only a few kids in shop knew the difference. Hoods they were called and carried chains their older brothers used in what gangs the town had ten years earlier. The way of the hippie, not the hood, that's what's hip, according to those pot-smoking people, the cult of said hippiness about to engulf everyone who was not joining up to use napalm. Get with it, the movie crew said, with their slouching around, but they worked so hard slouching day and night that they hardly ever did anything so dull as eat.

That left kissing. Basically ever since the movie people came to town, that was our major preoccupation: puckering up to look like Robert Duvall when he saw the pancakes my sister put down in front of him at Mrs. Berry's. I have the munchies, he said and made that face.

That kind of love we understood—but why call the movie *Rain People*? Our town was in the middle of droughtsville, a nowhere place with not a drop of rain for at least a month at a time, going on two, the limit to what we could remember backwards given our beer-drinking habits. Still, being underage, things were often dry in that regard, as well as weather-wise. Even the alfalfa beaten under all that irrigated water looked thirsty. But we feared asking the director our too-dumb question. He had a beard and a loud voice and we were wannabe extras. We feared even chatting with the principals while they ate their Mrs. Berry's or swam nude at the public pool at midnight or wore loose cotton dresses that let you see their tits through their armholes.

What we did know was that a payphone was important to the script, especially the payphone in front of the one-night-stand hotel that housed on its patio an actual row of tricycles resulting from various more permanent stands that had turned into monthlies. Kenny lived there with his mother who had romanced nearly every single dad in town but her yen was for the least attractive. Voted ugliest guy in the class, Kenny had a toad's mouth and chin and small eyes, though he was smart. Maybe his father was from out of town. Usually he worked nights at the hotel, washing the coffeemaker in reception and other low-profile chores, but he loitered around the set so much and into the shots that the director cast him. We were agog with envy. Not the high school sweetheart, chisel-chinned Max? Not cheerleader Sally whose hair never moved an iota even in a stiff prairie breeze? Or LuAnn, who let her coat fall open whenever the director went by so he could see the bikini underneath even though the weather was practically February? She said her mother insisted but nobody believed her. What Kenny had to do inside that payphone was pretend to talk a long time while the actress cried and beat on its glass, begging him for her turn while somebody's dad-turned-volunteer gladly swept water from a firehouse over her front with those eye-popping nipples.

What Kenny did full time was fancy himself a lover, especially with regard to one girl who couldn't care less. He said he was picking up tips from the movie people in this regard, that they took up with each other every night in their rooms and out of them, in different couple-combinations. A lot of fresh sheets, he said, almost mortified. There was a contingent of us who didn't know why.

Anyway, after the payphone scene was shot twenty times, Francis Ford Coppola—*like a cop* he told the actress and she said *like cop a feel?* and took a drag on the bud, laughing—directed like a cop, loud and short, and said cut, cut, cut just when Kenny was about to unfold the door. By then the actress had already left for her hotel room shivering from her shower, a beer shoved in her hand, so as soon as they moved the camera, we all piled into the phone booth with Kenny. It was the era of piling: Volkswagen bugs with dozens of kids stuffed inside, really as many as could fit in whatever car the owner didn't mind getting scarred up by legs kicking or fingernails clutching at the upholstery while people screamed *air! gimme air!* and laughed while the newspapers and the radios told of all the bad things that could happen in such a setup, and what was a record. Thirteen of us managed to squeeze inside that phone booth, the last girl, the one Kenny was in love with on top, held there by Kenny and probably six other guys who wanted to touch whatever parts of her that came their way. It was like a game of Twister, another excuse for mauling girls. Thirteen of us altogether inside it, probably half of them female, but all of us unlucky because, yes, when we couldn't get the door open and had to rock it hard, the booth fell over and broke. Nobody got cut too bad, although some girl, maybe the one Kenny liked, did step on his face hard. Since Coppola had paid him $20 cash, Kenny bought everybody ice cream from the hotel vending machine and nobody sued. My dad was the county attorney so I know. The movie people did consult him, however, about getting a bunch of them off charges of drinking and driving that the sheriff had slapped them with. He managed to lessen the sentence to community service, so all the production had to do was clean up the fake set stuff they had strewn across Main Street to make it look even worse than it already was. The director settled the matter like a macho Italian, Dad told us, giving him a bottle of wine, although he came from Detroit and had polio. Then the crew skipped town, leaving the mess in the street, hightailing it to Tennessee to finish the film where drinking and driving was less of a problem.

But Kenny had touched his goddess in the phone booth. On that high, he asked her to the prom a few weeks later. When she refused, he drove his two-cylinder Honda off the end of the unfinished interstate in the middle of a drag race, while the rest of us stopped at the quarter mark and watched in shock. He just rode on and on, both arms outstretched like a guy on a crucifix. The bike motor roared at the end of the road and then we heard nothing and then crash.

Hardly anybody liked the movie but Coppola and his friend George Lucas who was always sucking up to him and sticking a camera around his camera went on to become the two most famous bearded guys in Hollywood. We never used the phone booth again, not even for calling long distance to guys we didn't want our mothers to know about, but the repaired one still stands, a monument to Kenny because what do you think he was doing while the water poured down on the actress outside but practicing his prom date call, over and over, better each take, he had bragged, much much better.

Mr. Schmeckler

Very intellectual, says Polly. The rollers in her hair, a dozen frozen-juice cans, make the satirical bob that follows dragonesque and fierce. It's hopeless? I shuffle the pages of my paper in order, out of order. Polly uses an index finger to slide a single sheet out of the stack. The sad part is that it could have been any sheet, a fact Polly soon shares, pointing here and there in critique.

I scramble to note every comment. I forgive her tone—a self-reflexive slip, really, how she covers her genius with generosity. We work until daylight, until I'm caffeine-shaky at the keys and she's fixing footnotes. She lies across my bed, her long dark hair unspooling off the rollers, her fairest-of-them-all skin surrounding "devouring eyes"—an English-class description—not to mention a set of knockers the covers only half-cover, nightgowns for her being too bourgeois and confining. I myself am wrapping my shoulders in a *ruana*, the South American blanket I wear to make my nightgown look like a peasant skirt—that is to say, to look like I'm dressed—when Dad calls.

She picks up. Mr. Schmeckler? They laugh, Dad just as amused by her pet name for him as she is, he being more Irish than Easter—his phrase. They chat and she doesn't say a word about how hard she's worked all night for his errant daughter—her phrase—while I stir the discarded orange-juice cans in search of a paper clip.

They're arriving at three, she says in a beat, hanging up.

You could, like, let me talk too, I say over my toothbrush.

She casts her eyes up, where Somebody is surely noting my obtuseness. You were busy.

Okay, so I have to head out fast, get the paper to the prof's actual house before the cock crows, as it were. At the threshold, Polly yells that we should get my parents to take us to Bunny's after graduation. The prof treated her there last week, and she loved it.

It's like electricity, the way she loves and wants you in on it, a straight connection. It's a girls' college we're going to, but guys—maintenance all the way to department heads—know her name, they get the electricity too. With her by my side, I'm not just another Mick on a scholarship. I can't finish papers for the life of me, but my analysis is great, or so she says.

My *ruana* sweeps the dew and I break into a run. If I can get a decent grade for this, Polly and I will be Two Broads Abroad again this summer in England, a fellowship for her and teaching English to Asians for me—don't ask. Last summer we drank beer in Munich and did her prof's research. That's when Dad took on this Schmeckler name. He showed up with flowers for us around August, just when we were running low on the stipend, about six marks short of giving up and flying home. I was surprised. Dad had never showed up before. I mean, he'd never made any graduation of mine or my brother's, he was always working so hard, but last summer he was riding the 60s high on a contract for explosive bolts, something neither of us wanted to know about, being practically professional protesters of anything explosive. In honor of his arrival in Munich, Polly kicked out the schnitzel-eating un-exchanged student—that's what she called him—she was sleeping with. For virginity's sake, she said, even though Dad had already walked into our dorm room once at school when it was overpopulated.

Mr. Schmeckler's sitting on my bed when I return, out of breath, from the prof's house.

Where's Mom?

She had an appointment. To get her hair done. His face goes ablaze with an Irish blush. We're divorcing, he says, as if that's what Mom's hair-doing is really for.

I take Polly's bed. Catholics can't get a divorce, I say.

Mom—

Polly walks in. My Indian blouse looks great on her without a bra, eggs sunny-side up with nipples. Her big smile for Dad changes, seeing me.

At dinner they talk about the Vietnam War, how Johnson is bluffing, how contracts for bolts are increasing, and how evil Dad is, given that any contract will involve defense money. But the bolts protect the boys, he pleads to Polly, who is adamant that all manufacturing of anything out of that budget hurts someone. It's all entwined, she says, ordering another drink for herself. They drink a lot, and so do I. The three of us are loud enough that on our way back, the watchman at the school gate reprimands us, but not Dad.

I fall asleep on my bed without turning off my light.

He leaves, and Mom doesn't call. I can't believe it. I am going to England for months, maybe even a year, and she doesn't even want to say goodbye, or tell me what's going on. Polly says not to call her, it isn't my place, a mother's supposed to console the daughter in a divorce. After all, I am the hurt one, whilst they go on their merry ways.

Dad doesn't show up in Europe this time, nor in the fall we decide to stay on for. Polly gets me through. We eat toad-in-the-hole and date Oxford men, and I find one that Polly tolerates, though he's Tasmanian, not really English. Of course, a devil. We marry during a bright patch of winter on a hillside in Spain, with Polly at my side, along with the prof who supervised her independent study, and several just-sheared sheep. My parents pitch in for the honeymoon in France but don't show, singly or together.

Polly could take the prof home but flies back to grad school instead, the one he helped her get into. When I return, I enroll for a law degree and don't see my parents for another three months, not until my brother calls me to report that my mother has taken to her bed. I visit and she's so ill she can't even make me pancakes. I stay with my father instead, and his new wife, two years my junior. He sits me down in their living room and makes me read the divorce papers as a test of the new legal knowledge he is paying for. He wants to see if old Mr. McKibben, his lawyer, is up-to-date.

What I learn is this: Dad and his new wife now own this large house on the Cape and they want for nothing. My mother, one foot in the grave, wants. The document's formal tone can't hide her diminishment. While I page through it, I wonder at my own newly married state and how little I know of its future petitions and adjournments. I almost don't read to the end, which, in a brief, is the beginning, where the facts, such as they are, are depositioned. Maybe I know them already and don't want to read them.

Polly is named.

Of course he can't tell me himself. I look around at the chintz coverings, the wicker and glass, seeing nothing. By insisting I read these papers, is he trying to warn me away from Polly? Or get even with Polly by hurting me? Or am I guilty too now, knowing about it, since she is my friend?

It looks good to me, I tell him.

How happy Dad had been to visit me in schnitzel-land, staying three extra days.

A year later Polly hears that I'm back in town with a position, not practicing law but close to it, teaching it not far from her grad school. We sit at a table with a bottle of wine between us, and a husband each to drink it. We speak of solemn things, all the dead in the war so far, the iconic picture of the man holding a pistol to another man's head, the Beatles' breakup. I bring up this last topic, feeling brazen by the bottle's draining, feeling I can lower the tone and open the dialogue with the terrible shattering of the Fab Four's friendship over what, a mere Love-In girlfriend?

The two men have begun a side chat about guy trivia, stocks, like they care, and varieties of woods-of-the-world, her guy being a carpenter who is building her a huge house out of lumber he steals from the sites he works on. My Tasmanian admires his moxie, but their conversation lulls with my Beatles trivia, which opens a big, quiet hole.

It was like a marriage, the Beatles had a contract, I say, the law-yer in me still so new. The breakup of the century. Yoko betrayed them all.

I'm sorry, Polly says out of nowhere.

I hadn't believed what I had read in the divorce papers until then. I was certain my mother had fabricated everything, my sick mother without a new mate and an expensive porch overlooking the ocean. When I called her on her birthday, she couldn't say anything, her nurse very gently hanging up on me. Now, nothing graceful or forgiving is ever again going to come out of my mouth in answer.

We were best friends, is what I say. Before she can color that with something consoling, I head toward the ladies' but I find the front door instead, and sit in the car until my husband locates me, as husbands are wont to do, on a hunch. I don't cry, although decades later my shrink says I should have.

Polly persists. She wants the last word, she wants more than that, she wants our friendship to continue, as a sign of my forgiveness. But by associating with Polly, I caused the divorce and thus my mother's illness, and when she dies, my mother leaves what she has to my brother. Somehow Polly sees the obit and sends a condolence note. She also sends me birthday and Christmas presents, with *Love* in the note that's tucked into whatever. We still share friends from college, and once we bump into each other by accident. I see she has the Clintonian drive: if one person at a party resists her, that's the one she must amuse. I resist—and she showers me with wit and concern. Who else knows me so well, and so relentlessly? Then, because my mother, who didn't know me at all, is so dead, I invite Polly to the Cape while my father is away.

She has divorced the carpenter—he finished the house—and found a research partner from South Africa, a woman with whom she shares no history, who can write with her, Polly having, via osmosis with me, I suppose, become unable to finish her own academic papers, and she invites her and the woman's husband along. Buffers, I decide, being tentative myself but in thrall to the outrageousness of my invitation, and hers. The woman and Polly are more intimate than I expect, what with academic sighs that develop into sleights-of-conversation I can't quite follow, the two of them shouting at each other from their Schwinns as we round one more lovely bluff view of the Cape. Their topic is geography, how humans have to share it, and they're popularizing it with their magnum opus, *Down with Capitalism*. Even with my advanced degree, theory like theirs is too thick.

We kick-stand our bikes at the beach, a long one with crashing waves and surfboards. While the South African and her husband and mine run down to the water, Polly and I nick our knees up under our chins, waiting for water-awe to subside. Polly closes her eyes. I don't know what you're up to, she says to me.

How about you, with your ex? I say.

I'm talking about the whole world, and you in it.

I write a word in the sand with my toe, who knows what—harbor, as in feelings? It's too long a word to be hate. I'm so suddenly happy she sees me.

Temporary Autonomous Zone, Polly shouts, seeing the others dragging back driftwood. Together we build a little kingdom in the sand with the wood, and roll over—how does it always happen?—a rock throne for her to sit on.

Polly dies before my father does, asphyxiating on a plane in the middle of an intellectual point, a peanut stuck in her windpipe.

My father, out-Schmecklered by his newest wife, does not say, *How fitting*. I do not know if he cast Polly away so many years ago, or if the divorce lawyer said to cool it, and cooled, Polly never returned. Or perhaps she did return. I do not ask. I stand on his porch after telling him the news, facing the water Polly and I had watched together, eating its way up the beach toward him.

She was my friend then and forever, and whatever he thinks to say about her, he is not worthy to say it.

80s Lilies

The calla lilies in New Zealand say we are dead, just step off the jade-strewn, rimed high-tide line here and a wave will rise up like Trigger, like some silent movie stallion, and suck us under, suck us beneath a continental shelf stuck out so far the waves whiten before they break. So too the calla lilies, all white and wild like that, all about to break in the greeny drizzle that the wind whips, all these wild calla lilies will bear us away.

I see the lilies and I say, Let's get off the bus. Then the bus's burring keeps on without us as we stand at the upper ridge of lilies, before they spill off the grave mounds corralled by wooden fences and multiply right on into the waves. Lilies from old settlers' tombs, I say into the silencing wind with you tucking the baby onto my back and as far as we can see, green drizzle, jade beaches, white cups in clumps flattened by wind.

Mind the waves, she says. They will jump the beach and pull you in.

She comes abreast of us, nearly green-skinned in the green mist with a small-sized boy just as green, tugging at the end of her arm. Does she mean for us to mind those waves—or him, the green monkey among the lilies?

I hold up a rock. Jade? Really jade? I ask.

Tourists, she says in a tone that can't be confused. Tourists don't come here, she says.

Really? They skip this bit? I thumb toward all that various beauty. Those terrible tourists.

She laughs and my husband and I say all the little things against the wind that make her lean toward us down the length of the beach until we are at her car that she unlocks and leaves in, waving. We wave back, a few more little things on our lips.

The baby takes away our wonder at the place and its people, the baby has his wants. At the end of the road the woman has driven away from sits a pub, curiously free of all the lilies, as if bulldozed free. We order pints there, we ask after rooms since the green mist can only give way to dark.

They have rooms.

We remark on the sheep smell of these rooms, and the drizzle-colored pub interior, its darts bent and broken, the dark growlings and the stares from the pub fiends, two steamy goldminers, silent and filthy in their mining gear, flakes of dirt green not gold falling from them onto their table, and we order another pint.

Going to the ladies, with the baby asleep, milk lip aquiver, I trip over huge bones in the corridor, vast gnarled, prehistoric big gray bones that must be the source of the sheep stink. The dog that gnaws at such bones, as terrible an animal as that, thumps and growls from inside some further door when I shut mine. He's quiet when I emerge, as if he has plans.

I haven't. I haven't said Yes yet to the room or to another pint. I just want to talk about those bones but at our seat there's no one to note my near miss with the bone-guarding dog, no man nor child.

One of the two miners nods to the window, Out there. She has them in her car.

Where else would you be putting up but here? she shouts over new pell-mell rain. I have tea, she says.

We rode the ferry that sinks, the ferry with a crèche where the children are roped to rockers through the big waves that slap the island apart, the ferry that, however, did not sink when we crossed but allowed us, vomitous, to board that bus to here.

That ferry's no problem, she says. Look in the phonebook.

I open the phonebook and the first page lists all the calamities:

tidal wave, earthquake, floods, volcanic eruptions, and numbers to call. Such a safe place, I say they say, so safe for children.

We are fleeing, we explain, to some safe place. We're sure this time they'll drop it. We thought, Here's a place we'll be safe and gave the airlines our gold card.

They don't laugh, she and her husband. Just the way she doesn't laugh at the green rock I pull out of my bag, the rock, I say, that must be worth money. Their house is full of toys my baby knows and toys my husband can feel the remote of, and books I have read and admired. Her husband has my husband's charm and why not? They do nothing similar for work but charm makes the men match.

The baby inspects all the toys their boy brings so I can talk while she cooks because cooking is the point of visiting, isn't it, she says, a place where everyone meets. Then you can go back, if you like. After tea.

I look out into the pell-mell greeny rain and even in the looking, smell sheep, hear that growl. When real night falls about two drinks after tea—what is surely dinner—when the rain isn't seen but felt, they won't let us go, they make up beds.

Their boy bounces a ball off the baby's head and the baby smiles.

We visit a goldmine in the morning, their idea.

They're so nice. Maybe they wanted to have sex with us, I whisper to my husband as he settles a hard hat onto his head.

A little late, he says.

We walk deep into the mines posted *Do Not Enter* and they say, Don't mind the signs, the baby is fine.

This is where we're going when it happens, says her husband. Then he explains what he heard on the bar's TV yesterday, how it will blow ash all over the globe in ways nobody knows. Everywhere will be caught in the grip of its terrible winter.

Winter—you are obsessed with having seasons that don't match ours, I say to them. I look at my husband. So here is not safe either, says my glance.

We walk along in the dark.

I expect a room of gold all aglitter at the end, jutting ore burnished to a sun's strength. What we get to is a small cave lit with mirrors which leave little flashes of faraway light on the dull rock.

Our faces facing the mirrors are just one gray ball, then another.

Their boy drops a rock down a shaft and it doesn't hit bottom. While we wait, the baby wakes as if the rock hits hard, and his wails echo all down the tunnel. We walk back through his wails, it's that physical.

We stay one more night. We stay up late and my husband says, Maybe the threat will blow over.

Blow over. We all laugh, drinking wine from the grapes that grow among the lilies. Then we talk movies, all the same ones we have seen as if together.

We really came to see you, I say. Does it matter if we flee if you are here?

In the morning they tell us they do not write, they will not. No letters.

Consider them written, says my husband.

We take the next bus, a dark cave filled with more miners abandoning mines. The settlers we leave behind, such settlers as they are, wearing our clothes nearly exactly, franchise for franchise, wave as our bus burrs off past the lilies, the big waves behind them lapping and reaching.

Read the Snow

It tastes like this, he says, try it. He swallows more hotel pool water. His brother says it doesn't taste like that, she drinks Coke with it. He splashes him, hoping Mom will hear from that high window and what?—galoomph his brother, at least with her eyes. He splashes more until he sees no one's behind the splashing, that his brother has sunk and swum.

He lies back in the water to get a load of sun. It is too far to cross the pool in pursuit and his stomach has that cool feeling of vomit-to-be from all the swallows he's made. He could vomit if he wants to or he could even pull off his suit—the pool people who clean it every time anyone gets in have skipped, not one maid is hanging around with a feather baton to tell them to pipe down in chopped-up English. This makes him miss Mom more—why can't she come down?—so he flips and swims and butts his brother in the back with his head.

His dad has flown home early.

Loud planes cross the courtyard's square of sky, as old as the tiny ones he's painted the wings of. Bad engines, he says to his coughing brother who has splashed a sort of question.

The whole country's breaking-down-noisy. Diesel from the half-dead bus on the plaza ruined their outdoor lunch the day before. He dogpaddles into the really deep part. Not that Mom hadn't already ruined lunch by not eating, just ordering Cuban sandwiches that she only eats the pickle out of, and only drinking pink or brown drinks—his brother is right about the Coke—one after another as soon as Dad left in his taxi.

His brother bites him hard from out of nowhere, draws blood, and he kicks his brother back, in the gut, one, two—and gets out at the first set of steps. It's too annoying to swim and be bleeding. He shouts back at his brother: Leave me alone, just leave me alone, and one of the planes overhead swoops and drops a lot of flyers.

One of them falls on his back-floating brother's chest. Seeing his brother flail, he laughs so hard he almost slips on the cement. Nice, he says, watching the black ink swirl in the water. Most of the rest of the flyers sink and their ink bleeds straight out. He grabs one caught in a potted palm. Of course it's all in Spanish. Of course Dad could read it, but where is Dad? Home already.

He pulls open the door.

You can't leave, says his brother. We have to buddy.

The pool's a mess, he says, and exits before his brother can climb out and see all the ink on his chest.

In Cuba, says the ambassador, and he stops. He's always saying that. This country he's in couldn't have a revolution if it wanted to, if an eagle ate a revolution over their heads and shit it. Why, just before the elections—he stops again, pen poised over his journal that is going to make him famous someday so that Batista can appoint him to some better country, he stops to admire his niece who is playing the piano off the courtyard. She's playing something womanly, that is, something that makes her breasts jiggle and her thighs shift over the bench.

Behind him, and not for the first time, his maid curses. Bits of paper fall all over the patio, swirl down out of a perfectly blue sky, and quite a bit of them lodge in the second-rate foliage of this so-called republic. The maid curses and steps from the shadows to sweep at the fallen paper, to brush the tiny bits into a pile and pluck the strays from her broom while muttering, leaning back to stare into the sky.

High in the citadel behind my house, he writes, is where this benighted country locks up anyone who thinks anything.

He changes that to something sweeter. The maid is sweeping the patio too often, often right behind him. Close all the windows, he says to her in such a sugared voice, as sweet as one from the cane fields, from the trading floors of the rubber barons, from the well-pleased dictator nearby. He whispers it softly so she will have to come near and exhibit her décolleté to him, bending at the sill. Close the windows, he whispers, and tell my niece to play with a little more vigor.

A carbine, he decides. Carbine, he says to his brother who slaps his wet bare feet on the tile behind him. The soldier holds a carbine at the end of the hall, the first hotel person they've seen between the pool and their mom's room, and the gun is the real thing. We have a key, he tells the soldier when they are close enough to really admire the gun, and when you look right at him, he is the nervous kind of soldier, his fingers up at his mustache, down at the gun. I have the room key, he says. He holds it up. The soldier backs off, lets him use it.

Mom has half her black sequin-and-fluff dress crushed inside his brother's suitcase. You're bleeding, she screeches, the way she does when she drinks, high and happy.

Yes, he says, it's nothing he says, to belittle his brother who is not going to say he did it, who is pushing into the room right behind him.

Oh, well—just another surprise for your father, says Mom. Your father may have important things to attend to that he can't finish a vacation for, but so does this country. We have to go now too.

No, he says. We can't go back now. So soon?

She gives him a look. She smiles at his brother who could be smirking, then shrieks: Ink! All over you. Don't touch anything!

While she rushes her high-heeled slippers into the bathroom for a towel, he drops the flyer he found stuck in the potted plant into the suitcase. Really, it's his only souvenir except for the plastic daggers that came with her drinks the night before. Mom had gone on drinking and dancing after Dad left, arching her neck like a swan against one of the dancers you pay for that Dad had made fun of, or else maybe it was one of Dad's magazine friends who so often show up on what they call junkets.

His brother is sneaking a sip from Mom's glass even though it is lipstick-stained-icky. He is taking a big gulp just as she throws a towel at him and shrieks, We've got to get going, and beats the suitcase closed.

The soldier is still in the hall when she flounces out, arm in arm with him as if he is Dad, and his brother is carrying both suitcases. The soldier lets them know that he has to search their things before they go anywhere or anyway that's what he does, never mind what he says. As the soldier shakes open her suitcase, his mother says, Revolution, my goodness, does it count duty free too?

His niece says, It is not that important, or that's what she says beforehand but afterward, standing at the courtyard door in his robe, she cries so he knows it is something indeed, maybe her first. Standing beside her, he's wondering about her age—she came to him after she graduated, after her father had been executed already two years— when the paper bits begin to fall again, this time falling into the roses and he thinks of the War of Roses and the diplomatic maneuvers that prolonged it and of the thorns that they used on the prisoners who ended up in oubliettes and of course of the crown of Christ, who does not grace this country's capital in a hundred-foot-tall statue over the port but could, if this country were only a little more involved in the oil boom. The girl breaks into his thoughts with a sob and he finds a chocolate for her from the silver box on his desk, but not before he closes the door to block out the sound of sirens on the road up to the citadel.

Propagandista, shouts the soldier, snatching the flyer out of the suitcase.

This is not propaganda, Mom says, putting on her glasses. Let me see. She leans close to the carbine and pretends to translate. It says here we must go—nothing about execution. No executions, she points at him. What about a tip?

He can't help it, he vomits at the soldier's feet.

See what you've done to my son, she says to the soldier. My son, she shrieks, catching him in the crook of her arm, the half-closed suitcase in the other. He's sick and I must leave, she says. I've got a plane to catch.

The soldier cleans off his shoes with the flyer, he doesn't stop us.

The niece is sunbathing on her back when the paper bits fall the third time. She is sure what she glimpses is something from a bird so she doesn't brush off the one that falls on her blanket right away, she touches it and in her relief that it is not wet, she lifts it to her face. She is not as myopic as her uncle thinks or as myopic as he pretends he is, the way he's missed the gearshift more than once, gripping her knee instead. For a few moments she holds the paper at arm's length as a shade, a piece small enough to cover one lid, with just the word *Ayuda!* written in the tiniest script over and over.

Help.

She sits up.

She picks other bits out of the rose bushes and they are all the same, *Ayuda!* written in a woman's hand, perhaps the one she saw waving from the citadel that shades their courtyard so completely for two hours every afternoon that she is forced to sun in the morning.

The maid scurries out to sweep them up. She says Si, all the papers falling say the same, but when the niece asks her to read one, she can't.

Some woman is cracking ice cubes out of the tray in the kitchen as if she has always done that, as if she has come into their apartment just to do that. She is somebody he has seen at a party he has had to shake hands with, some woman in one of those furs with the animals' heads still on and biting each other at the clasp, and that woman is the one now standing in her—well, in fact, Mom's robe—asking if they want to have a drink and talk about it.

They're home two days too early.

If only, he says to his brother, looking back, if only those flyers had fallen, say, even a day later and the revolution had begun closer to when we were originally supposed to leave then Dad would have left with us and all the way back to the apartment Mom would have needled him only about working too hard, coming back so early.

He'd have a dad today without that revolution.

Women mill past them in tight black dresses, becoming and unbecoming. They are greeted. The minister takes another sip of his cocktail. You must be very happy to have your niece with you.

Here she is, says the ambassador, the aspiring pianist.

Wearing a dark cowl around her face in the style of the day and her mood, his niece lifts her hand for a kiss, with such eyes. As soon as she ghosts off, the minister says, my wife has disappeared.

The ambassador is very circumspect, he ducks his head when he hears *my wife*, he says, It is such a small country, she must be very skillful to disappear.

Yes, says the minister. Very skillful.

They drink with their heads tipped over their glasses and their elbows akimbo, as if they are thirsty birds. She was a writer, says the minister. Is a writer, he says. I miss her. He casts a look upward, toward the citadel.

Knife Block

I've always had a knife, he says, jabbing it toward his father. And the guys in the guest room are my friends.

He's twenty-five, not six years old, and this is not a Swiss Army knife forced out of its sheath with baby teeth, but a large piece of kitchenware pulled out of a block. His friends are also large and draped over the spare bedroom's bed, chair, rug, and window seat— four of them, one a girl. They stink but one of them is less homeless than the others because he still has a phone which means he can be reached, which is all home means really is what she's thinking, the stepmom behind the father who, so quiet in the kitchen–*he has guests!*—found the knife stuck deep into the breadboard instead of the block. His son, embarrassed, has pulled it out.

No biggie, says her stepson, except that he lunges at his dad, a guy who is ex-Marine and thick-trunked and dodges well, but trips.

Yesterday the social worker said she could intervene only if they got hurt. Is that now? The dad on the floor—*I'm okay*, he says—holds his palm out for the knife. The son considers the offer, clenching it upright, his knuckles white around the handle.

One of his new friends bumps up behind him and says, Man, you need the jaggedy one to cut toast.

I ate all the bread, says the son. He casually sheathes the knife back in its block. While his stepmom helps his dad off the floor, the rest of the loungers appear at the guest-room door, prepared for exit, but not before a quick tour of the kitchen. One of them pulls out the knife again and checks its edge, the one with the phone says, Thanks for the sleepover, and the girl takes the rest of the bananas.

So much like his father in girth and width and height, born late in his father's life, the boy always had problems, but his brother grew up to be a suicide. His real mother had something to do with that, at least in the way of genes. Even at four, he managed to walk into traffic, at six, mix cocktails of vitamins and her weight-loss pills, at nine, cut his arm with his brother's first dull-bladed pocketknife. Nobody would give a knife to him, not to bolster his manhood or whittle or take apart a lock. Now that he is dead, this older son has dibs on total preciousness.

The next day the stepmom drives past the party the homeless are having beside the Taco Bell. The whole town knows not to frequent that alley. After several hours spent convincing the pharmaceutical powers-that-be that she needs access to her stepson's prescriptions, that more time without the meds just makes him crazier, that she is not going to swallow them, just deliver them, they hand over a bagful. Just why was that transaction so hard when it was so easy for the hospital to release him after only three days of observation? Protecting his rights, they said.

Protection is what she needs, the covers pulled up over her head. She is way past seventy-five now, not so spry, and her stepson is putting on muscle lifting the fridge at 3 a.m. for rats the size of his fist, he says, and to catch aliens who stay cold underneath.

Yes, Adult Protective Services exists but its wheels, says her husband, are mired in legalities. We will be jelly from lack of sleep, if not stabbed dead in our beds by the time they come into play.

Depression always follows the boy's mania, that is their hope, and it has saved them before. The swing has always been predictable and quick, but also correctable by medication, when he takes it. Every few months, he breaks down enough for them to call an ambulance and have him carted away for a psych evaluation so she and her husband can have the three days of observation off, without the pots and pans hauled out in the middle of the night, "freed" from their cupboards, the cereal sprinkled on the carpet with milk and sugar, the cat that he actually loves put in the trash can for "eavesdropping." This time, however, aided and abetted by his doctor being on vacation and the lament *I really have no friends* alternating with the recitation of all of Marvel comics history, frame by frame, he doesn't tell them for days that he lost his meds in a game with these so-friendly poker-playing homeless kids.

His friends have wizards for parents and eat squirrel when they have to, or so they boast. The phone kid, whose phone turns out to have been merely ornamental since his parents aren't paying for it anymore—no more calls to Russia, or the Antarctic, he tells the stepmom when she asks for the number after delivering the meds. The letters are numbers, he says, S-U-C-K-E-R, he spells out. He does have a squirrel tail attached to his backpack.

Her stepson runs off between cars with the bag of meds. Wait, she yells after him. I have something to tell you.

The friends laugh, the guy with the phone offers his phone.

She is shaking when she finds him again an hour later, hidden behind a large air-conditioning unit beside the railroad station. Every bit of her thin frame's in motion. Confronting him is her idea. Go ahead, said her husband, let him have it. He is old enough now, say it to his face, maybe it will change something.

Her husband doesn't believe in change.

I can't live with you anymore, she says to her stepson. Get out of my life. Don't ever come home.

After nearly twenty years of mothering, all these terrible words rush out.

He weeps. His birth mother rejected him years ago—and now his own stepmother? Really, it is his home too, his house, his dad made it, he weeps, he even helped him put in the front step's cement, the one that keeps the president-elect from telephoning the alien Galaxy Masters for help because it is so dense with sand and whatever else cement is made of that there is plenty of room for all the battalions.

She walks back to the car, sobbing too, one step as heavy as the next, as if she weighs a thousand pounds. No wonder she can't eat.

You are not my son, rehearses his father. He can't get the words out. They live in Arizona where the desert dries every syllable, the few he manages to say inside their car that is parked in the lot of the Taco Bell. It is much harder for him to do this than her, he tells her. His tongue is thick with trying and Taco Bell rhymes with fucking hell and that's what we're in, a hell of a situation, but he doesn't want his son or the homeless to hear him say that or they win. Their son hears more than is said anyway, said the social worker at their meeting an hour earlier. He should have a little (big?) wall between what he says and what he thinks, and nothing but medicine can put it up again. He's an immigrant in his own head.

We need a plan, his father says, and they drive home.

That night the stepson brings home six new homeless friends. What did it matter what she'd said? She and his father say nothing but they have not shopped, they have eaten elsewhere, they have showered, shaved, and locked themselves in their room. At 3 a.m. they hear a scream and the tumult of friends running away, the door slamming. When they peer out, their son is standing beside the door, twisted in fury. All summer I worked for that money, he shrieks.

One of the homeless asked for his bank password, and he gave it.

He made the saved money on his first real job, on a work crew in the sun, overseen by a friend of the family. He used a screw gun, and well. He recited the times tables and fit the screws neatly into the new ice-cream-store fence. He was so polite. Charming, said his employer. He always smiled, held the door for her, always listened, even to her retelling of dreams.

He's so angry about the lost money, he lunges at the cabinets with the kitchen knife. Or is he practicing for them?

They slam their door shut on his raving.

His father does not like the idea of calling the police on his own son. He is not exactly churchgoing himself, he knows about police with their arms and ammo, their tendency to kick people prone, to suffocate. He does not like the idea of men that size handling guns of any kind. Calling the police goes far beyond saying his son can't come home, he says, it's like saying he is not his son, it's painting him all over with no-son-ness, it makes him someone totally alien, someone who the police and the fucking police state can control. That he cannot do. No.

But he is not your son when he's like this, she says.

The police do not touch their holsters, they do not kick. Is there a disturbance here? asks the calm head policeman. The stepmom has talked to the social worker in advance, not knowing how wild he and the homeless could get that night, and she has prepped the precinct. He and his friends are arrested, though not without a lot of flailing and terrible names being called, curses that the police say are unwarranted, and do the son no good.

He's still your son, she says to him hours later when they are sitting in bed in the dark, completely wired, fearing he will be kept away only three days again—or maybe less, given a sentence is involved instead of a psychiatric evaluation—and then he really will come for them, unimaginably furious about their betrayal. But they fall to sleep anyway because what can you do? And in the morning, the father goes to the court to talk to the court-appointed lawyer and the judge.

His son appears thoroughly chastised by his night in jail. He begs his father to be let out. His father tells the judge that two months ago his son so charmed the staff at the last evaluation that they released him earlier than usual, far too early for the meds to take effect, and about how old the two of them are, and getting much older, without sleep. The boy just needs time in treatment, he says to the judge. Without more time, the meds won't work.

The father doesn't mention the knife. He smiles, he ducks his head, he uses his charm, everything the son has learned from him, exactly what his stepmom had been seduced by so long ago.

Even the judge is susceptible.

She's alone in the house, waiting for his return. He called her about the result of his meeting, jubilant, as if they'd what—gotten pregnant? He didn't think this remark was very funny. We're out on parole, he says. That's better.

She slides the knife back into the block with the others, then slides it out and puts it under her pillow. To sleep on? Too lumpy. She tucks it under the covers with just the tip showing.

Demented.

She carries it back to the kitchen and starts to cook.

White Supremacist

The white supremacist wasn't so white. A skater on Venice beach, he tanned, and tanned well. But he was white inside and out, the way white is, scared, you know, chicken? said my friend Jenna after he went to jail. He was her stepson's best friend, but she said her stepson was never scared.

I met the stepson when I flew in for a visit. He held himself chest-first, with a skater's lock, and he never met my eyes, partly because his bangs were so long. He was also a writer. We walked the dog to the beach, and Jenna pointed to his tag scrawled over half the retainer wall, another thing he did with his friend. Bombing she called it, serious graffiti. A middle-class thing, writers and skaters— parents with good cars and three bedrooms. Jenna lived in a squat ranch that had a courtyard full of succulents she was reviving. I said I was amazed they needed reviving—succulents live.

Jenna shook her head. You don't know.

All the time, the sound of the two skaters doing their moves in the driveway, *whump whump*. All the time, her fear of her stepson breaking an arm, a leg, his friend landing on him.

They are sick, said Jenna. Which means good in skater.

Her stepson had a record for theft and Jenna said his friend envied him for it. Weird, huh? Because of that record, her stepson had a woman who came to the house to sit next to him and a computer three times a week for two hours, sent by the Board of Ed. I saw her at work that afternoon. She had a clipboard, lesson plans, and a mustache, and I don't know how she did it—how do you teach civics to a kid whose aim in life is to land a kickflip? She sat next to him as if they were going to play the piano together, and talked while she scrolled up and down on the computer. She said, Think of the computer as a refrigerator, with good stuff in it.

The stepson was really skinny. He was too tall and too thin and too smart to think of food. Everything that said *stop* in other kids meant *start* to him. He had a big brother who broke down now and then and took medication—not drugs, said Jenna—so he couldn't really skate or hang out with his brother. Jenna loved them both and you know how it is, she said, if you tell the younger one he can't have his friend over, he runs off for two days with his friend who also deals—to other people's parents.

I flew home with an education.

Jenna called often: the boy crashed their car, the boy wept in the bathroom, the boy stole brake fluid to thin his graffiti paint. Really, his brother with his mental problems was a piece of cake compared to him. At least they could drive him to the hospital.

I'd known Jenna for years. She was about as straight as they came: schoolteacher, museum job, manager of a pool for seniors, an exercise nut just like about everybody in California. We shared a love of pugs that survived their cross-country move. Her husband wasn't home often. Handsome and thoughtful, he liked to say he drank for a living but really he bought liquor for a conglomerate. Maybe he had other women or saw his first wife.

I was standing in a park, my pug tearing around, cellphone to my ear, wondering how things could get worse for her. The calls were like reports from a battlefield. Jenna started this one off by saying her stepson had a girlfriend. Which was good. The bad part Jenna said was that the girl tried to keep him from climbing this water tower he wanted to tag that his friend had dared him to and the guy stood at the bottom and forced the girl into kissing him while he was on his way up. At the top, he wrote CHKN for his friend and threw down the marker and made a sort of swan dive. Fifty feet.

My dog was barking like a maniac as if he could hear what she was saying. What's his condition? I said.

Okay, she said. He's got his cast propped on this special board. We've built a ramp for the front door. His friend has already been over with new chisel-tip Wite-Out.

She actually sounded cheerful then.

Her call three months later started: My stepson died yesterday.

A gallon of booze and then pills, she said in a stop-and-start voice. He was alive when he went to bed at 4 a.m. I heard him come in.

I never sleep anymore, she said.

She stopped.

I petted my dog so hard he yelped. Yes?

Okay, so, she said, not at all composed. He and his friend had been out looking for girls. That's what his friend said afterward to the police but I don't know, what kind of girls are around on a school night at that hour?

She made a very sad sound.

His friend hadn't taken the pills, she started up again, but he was with him all night and although her son came home alone, the kid snuck into the house to check up on him later.

I knew Jenna never locked her doors, I'd seen the damaged hardware. Both her sons broke in, the older one even broke out once in a fit of claustrophobia. She was always having to call the locksmith. She heard his friend tiptoe into his bedroom. Her stepson was still alive because she could hear them talk. She didn't know that he'd taken pills—booze yes, that was standard, maybe a few pills, not a whole bottle. As soon as she heard the kid leave, she got out of bed to pee and then stood at her stepson's door. It was already getting light.

He was the kind of kid who cleaned up well, she said, right? You remember?

I nodded into the phone. She wasn't really talking to me.

Or at least well enough that the Board of Ed sent that teacher to the house, she said: but he was never exactly cordial after a night out.

I didn't want to barge in. And, of course, he liked his privacy. She said she looked down at his door with the gouges all over that he'd made with his board, she put her hand on the knob and listened harder. It was the absolute silence that scared her. She turned the knob and went in, but she was too late. His lips were already a purplish blue. Like bruised, she said. The emergency people, by the time they showed, got out all their gear, but everybody knew it was for practice.

His friend could have told me, she said. There was time.

Right after she called, I had to drive somewhere with my husband. After my shock, my sympathy, and my condolences, I gathered up my checkbook, umbrella, and sweater. My pug rose to his haunches, a bit blind by now, but he trotted right out to the car, no coaxing.

My husband was backing out too fast. I screamed, but it was raining and the windows were rolled. I didn't throw my phone at the dog, afraid it would run under the wheel.

He had to get out of the car and shake me. The dog did not die.

Jenna called again minutes later. She was calmer. I forgot to tell you I told his brother and he didn't freak out. He's in a locked ward anyway, but only until Tuesday. And Mom is going into hospice and I might have to fly to Florida this weekend, and miss the celebration of life. I mean his funeral, she said.

Yeah, I found him, she said, as if I'd forgotten.

After saying *It's all right* over and over, even though no way in hell it was, I said, How is the dog? and she said she was almost finished walking him. He's old, she said. Like yours.

So what if Jenna wasn't the paradigm of mothering, she wasn't his mother, and maybe her stepson wasn't having any of it anyway.

Two years later Jenna read a newspaper with his friend's name in the headlines.

I had called her to tell her that my dog died.

Taken in a raid, she told me. The whole chinos and white shirts of Charlottesville? It would be like going straight for him. He was such a chicken. He would never run over the girl.

I could hear her dog barking at the other end, and her comforting him.

The kid will do time now, she said, laughing. She actually laughed at the idea. That was the one thing he envied: my son in jail. I'll bet he never even met a black person.

How can you not hate him? I asked. Not telling you about your sttepson when he could have been saved—and now this?

I don't know, she said after a while. Maybe it's that he reminds me of him? I don't have much that does.

I would hate him, I said.

I'm sorry about your dog, said Jenna.

Oxford

Right. Could be love. I did not say that aloud but instead hugged the waist of a boy called Graham, a name with a sigh built in, as he steered the motorbike I was trying not to fall from. I also wondered why what we were riding was called a motorbike here. Motorcycle sounded way cooler.

Thus my interests.

My parents had met a geography don from Oxford while he and his family were camping across the US, and he said I should come to his college and study there between terms. His wife offered their spare room. I didn't hesitate. I advanced a range of curriculum, the worst of which being witchcraft in the seventeenth century, and he, bless him, arranged a tutor in English philosophy.

Victory! shouted everyone piling out of the pubs in front of the motorbike, celebrating the win of the most important football game of the twentieth century—so far, Graham exulted. I'd had two gin and oranges, and Graham four. The celebrating horde made riding madness. We dismounted and inched forward through the honking and wild screaming and jets of beer shaken by fans, Graham walking his bike so masterfully around the drunks, while the don's son, Roger, revved his bike so close to ours I was afraid of a burn. I stuck out my hand to give us more room but Roger and then Graham fisted the air, thinking I was cheering.

Even more of a commotion broke out from the happy crowd as they lifted a bobby to their shoulders. While he flailed, you could see delight overcoming his disdain.

Bloody coppers, said Graham, who liked to go fast.

After an almost gluttonous Sunday afternoon when the don's wife served lamb and potatoes in crackling fat, a fare much superior to the usual cold supper of boiled egg and cold-buttered bread, I sat behind the curtain that provided the tiniest bit of privacy for the pantry shelf that I slept on, reinforced to bear the weight of ten kilo kegs of marmite and what appeared to be bottles and bottles of pickled tongue and just high enough that I couldn't touch the ground when seated. I sat uncomfortably for another reason: the inevitable bike burn. It's nothing, I told Roger while he searched for the ointment in his father's bathroom—did I actually say *nothing*? I barely suppressed tears. He had burnt himself in the past too, he said, as if comradeship made all the difference, and added that he always wore pants. This last he said as if my short skirt was stupid, but he very much enjoyed applying the ointment where I couldn't reach.

This had not escaped Graham's notice.

Graham had joined us in the pantry soon after Roger finished scraping the Sunday dinner plates. The pantry's curtains kept us slightly warmer than the rest of the house. The don turned off the heat after 3 p.m. *to keep the mind sharp*, he said, shouting at us on his way out for his Sunday walk. No, we chorused to his repeated requests for company, Not at all, said the son in fact, hoisting his math book toward his face as if proximity would yield understanding. The next time the don allowed heat would be at dawn after he delivered tea on trays to each bedroom the way a maid must've, fifty years earlier. If the hot tea did its magic, I could skip the trickle of cold water that passed for the shower and thrust myself, shivering, into frozen clothes. Heat from the coal bin crept up the stairs just as I fled the house to meet my tutor.

But it was still Sunday. Lying back on my shelf, I was ostensibly trying to write an essay on how having the brain of a person transplanted into another body might affect one's perception of the world. Roger sat to my right, his math text discarded as soon as the don hiked out of sight, and Graham doodled on a school-book on my left. He'd finished his O levels, he wasn't going to be bothered with philosophy, he'd brought over the joint. The more important question is which Beatle will go bald first, he said, trying not to exhale. After the two of them put a quid on Ringo, Graham interrupted Roger's thesis on how drumming affects the follicles by offering that loss of blood alone with a transplanted head might cause memory problems.

Very sensible, I said, and made a note.

I was hoping Roger's mother might announce the need for someone to clear the coal bin, as Roger was sitting too close to my burnt thigh. To distract myself further, I contemplated whether one could fall in love with someone whose head was transposed onto a different body. After all, Graham had a lovely broad-shouldered body and a headful of curls, while Roger's head was from his brilliant father, the don. But Graham's long lashes—

It was not Roger's mother who interrupted but Jane, his black-toothed older sister. Mail, she said, shoving envelopes through my curtains. Or shall I say, males? She inserted the rest of her head past the curtains while covering her mouth so you couldn't see her teeth while she laughed at the terribleness of her joke. She had nowhere to go since she'd failed her A levels and hadn't any expectations. We'd gone to a concert together once, where we talked rings, whether you could ever have too many, the most neutral subject I could broach vis-à-vis marriage. She could've delivered this mail from the box in town any time after two o'clock, when she usually went off to collect it, but no doubt having spotted Graham's motorbike outside, she made a special trip. She'd obviously forgotten to collect it on Saturday.

One envelope surely wanted tuition for college back home—I didn't care to open it—and the other was from my mother. The sooner I read it, the sooner Jane would leave. I tore it open. The two guys were still pretending we had a fly infestation with wild hand-flapping at the dope-filled smoke. My mother wants a special jelly no one has in the States, I said, reading. Lemon-grapefruit-kumquat.

Jane responded with a tight rodenty smile. Her just-as-tight pony-tail pulled her eyes at a slant: the word *plain* couldn't be helped.

My patience with her had dwindled but I needed to know where to find the jelly.

Tesco's, she said, a twenty-five-minute walk.

Not on the bike, said Graham. His arm was touching mine, with Roger staring past Jane as if she were part of the curtain pattern. Yes, I said. I had only another week left of my stay. Mother's jelly must be purchased and packed with the single china cup I'd bought to commemorate the trip, the paper on transposed heads finished, goodbye gifts found and wrapped, the goodbyes said and wept over. I shoved the envelopes to the back of my notebook. Anything else?

Jane stood silent beside the curtain, as if thinking. I was sandwiched between the two men, my notebook half-closed, and the two of them had slowly shifted, assuming even more chaste casual poses farther away from me. I shivered from the lack of contact and examined my burn bandage.

Jane took a seat on the other side of Graham, and asked after his mum.

I wouldn't know, he said. Ask mum, he said. He touched my hand.

I was surprised. A first.

Tea? said Jane, staring at the hands.

I'll make it, said Graham, acknowledging a stalemate. Roger nodded and the two of them fell off the platform into the kitchen, followed by Jane, who would supervise. I offered my souvenir cup with the queen overwhelmed by gold curlicues stamped on the side. The two men educated me on the finer points of tea making: the anatomy of the pot itself, its luscious curves and its long spout—sex-positive! exclaimed Graham—the necessity of "hotting" it up (much eyebrow lifting), the building pressure of the boiling, the obvious lust forcing the whistle.

They didn't say *lust*. While I giggled at the pantomime, Jane went off, disgusted, leaving the two of them to compete over pouring the tea into a cup from a height—like the Bedouins, said Roger. To bring up the froth.

I tidied up the spillage.

I had to concede that I quite liked Roger too, despite all the pimples on his forehead. Love? He was very good at math. Or maths, as

Roger corrected me, as if the numbers crowded around him, causing him to lisp. While he rummaged through the chaos at the back of the fridge for sugar, Graham said he used to steal the raisins here whenever he visited. She kept them under a box beneath the sink.

She liked to hide things from you too? I showed them where I found a small carton of milk—sitting outside on the sill, concealed by an overturned pot.

Mother thinks she's protecting it from birds, says Roger. What bird would peck through a carton?

My mother does the same thing, said Graham. It's to leave room in the fridge for all those cakes she never baked.

We drank every drop of milk.

I was to board the train at the hour the two of them usually tapped at my curtain, setting it aflutter, asking if I needed a gin, their motor-bikes at the ready. The need for liquids in this country, cold and hot, had been unrelenting. Graham took me to the station; Roger's exhaust had fallen off completely and he couldn't get his bike to start. Three on the bike was too many. I shook hands with the don and his wife and Jane, who wiped a tear from her cheek, and emphasized her allergies as the reason. Roger wouldn't look me in the eye while I shook his. The don gave me the eggshell of a bluebird he'd found on a walk and his wife produced a final piece of dry cake that she'd bought half price the previous winter and from which she'd been treating us with tiny squares for the last week.

Oh, Graham, I said at the station, and realized I'd never said his name aloud before. Goodbye.

Graham said nothing, which I intuited to mean, from other few near romances, everything.

Wasn't I in love with him? It was a narcissistic question; the better one was really, did he love me? I had taken that for granted. All those hours spent together in my pantry were clear confirmation. Was Roger his rival? They seemed more of a team. Or perhaps Jane rivaled me, with regard to Graham. Only once had he signaled that he noticed her by putting his hat on her head. How she had brightened to beautiful.

Jane wasn't as old as I thought. Her teeth fixed—bleached?—she now looked younger than me, ten years later, on another academic visit. I'd telephoned and she'd invited me to tea. Her parents had died, and Roger, off to live in the city as a stockbroker, said she should have the house. Had she fought for it? She still had the rodent smile, and she was still single. I admitted I hadn't a partner either, despite the toddler I'd brought along. He ate three of the beautiful petit fours, surely weeks old, that she presented on a piece of worn china, and then put his finger into hers.

Oh, have it, she said, so graciously. He didn't hesitate. And you might want to know what became of Graham?

I actually hadn't thought two minutes about Graham. He'd never returned a single letter of mine. I put that down to a general manly dislike of writing, his recognition of the distance between us, and, with regard to my impending philosophy degree, our divergent interests. Was I hurt by his silence? For several breathless months. I hadn't returned to her country to track him down, present myself with my foundling, and ask if he would take us to the pub, but still—what a good idea. He's got twelve children by now, I said. And they all drive little motorbikes in circles around him. Where's he gone to?

Jane couldn't help herself: her hand went up to shield me from her blinding teeth. He died a few months after you left. On his bike. A road accident.

That's why he didn't write, I said.

Exactly, said Jane. She couldn't hide how pleased that made her.

While I changed a diaper, I told her the jar that held the jelly I found for my mother had smashed my souvenir cup in the post. I had nothing to remind me of England except the burn scar on my leg.

We should keep in touch, she said, twisting her mouth into a smile.

Had Jane told the truth or was she preventing me from looking for him? That was my first response, wrangling the stroller through the door. I couldn't bear to ask her for details. So often that type of accident meant a terrible head injury. I sighted my own head cut off in shop windows. I imagined Graham without, blood gushing all over the road, but with no other body, and pushed the baby's stroller past all the bikes on High Street in sad ambulatory mourning.

Horses on My Side

The light is bad. Fields flee on either side of the car in gray-brown, a beaten color. Acceleration exists at the ball of his foot past each of these fields but he leaves off pressing so hard, preferring the gray-brown to the blur. Soon-moon, a kind of too-close rhyme, is how the twilight and the gray highway are going along with the fields, in an on and on that can only mean, in the end, Not so fast.

He doesn't speed up at all.

I'm waiting. I see him in the slow-motion hologram of familiarity, driving. He knows this and still he takes his time. He's coming, a lot in the -ing. I wait under the streetlight of the moon, and the half-cracked streetlight, and its corner with pavement I'm standing on, with no bus-shelter seat to tuck into. *Sure* isn't where I wait. I wait at the light as if he were arriving on a star from a long time ago, or in the dark of a bowling ball skipping lanes.

The car is another thing. It flickers its dials, expressing car disease, unaccompanied by a cure of any kind. Chug says our mode of transport, chug, chug. Yes, there are graceful turns, stops that seem crisp—but a car like this doesn't drive, it chugs and flickers, it expresses.

I wait with my soon-to-be-car-lit eyes, with worry a place in my head I keep close.

Earlier, to stay cheerful, I make bets with the kids on what they can count. We always did, brothers and sisters, backseat and front. Horses on my side was how we counted. But those pastoral exemplars now have duties other than highway, like glue factory or pageant parade or circling a $2 million TV wagon train. Besides, this isn't Virginia they're counting in or the livestock-infested West. Twenty points for palominos, they exclaim, but the most horses of any color they have seen are six. Still they will holler *How many?* if even a tail is spotted. Numbers drive them, not the godforsaken car—without horses, they tot up all kinds of states and statistics, exclaiming over each RI or HI plate, the shout itself keeping the gray of their passing at bay. The kids will count even plastic gas station mounts, they will count billboards of horses with grins. Or they will roll down the windows. Wind! they will shout, as if it's a number too. I can almost hear them; then, at last, I do.

I hold my head down for the getting in part and the plunge into the seat, and the car heaves out of the bad light with me inside it, among seatbelt flaps and the counting kids. Am I counted? To them, I'm a state plate already blurring in the distance, my entry's so suddenly over.

My husband ahems his greeting, a noise at the new cold of my entrance, which combines with the cold of the soon fully downed windows. Wind! the kids shout again and again, all glee. Cozying closer is not a simple operation for a driver, other than a commanding *Close It.* At stake is the car, an unsure vehicle for everyone together, a gamble within a driver's reach. Brakes R Us.

Of course someone answers I'm Hungry to his Close It, instead of Sorry.

What he does get is kissed. The one in back puckers up following her lot of electrical-window-up-and-down. This kiss doesn't lessen the anamorphic elsewhere travel is sucking us all into, it's just the smack in time that binds: he still exists. I kiss him good next and he almost misses the turn, the dark sign overhead, the bridge with the highway turning us off. But no, we keep careening into the sure dark all pecked up and smiling, and both kids declare their bliss. We bless the goofitis of the fat moon that brightens up even the bottoms of the hooves of all the horses they say they've missed, those bending to crop at a nightlight, dipping their faces into exhaust-covered feed or leaning on a fence as if they could break it, and lifting their legs.

I tell them my sister once spotted a giraffe in a horse trailer and we couldn't award her enough points.

A hundred points, shrieks the younger.

They say they have seen giraffes, just nobody else was watching. It's your fault, your glasses, they say, pointing at the pair sitting askew from all my kissing. I laugh, and we chug past the hillsides, into the towns we can't stop at because time and its horses don't count anymore, in such a dark.

Then I start with the bottles. How many bottles on the wall? I sing and they sing and we watch out the front and the sides and keep counting while the dark swallows us deeper, into the intestinal dark of some silent ruminant creature.

Rex Rhymes with It

I have flown home to harass my mother into living longer to spite Dad, who has been dead for some time now. She greets me with her who-cares look through her glass, tilted bottoms-up at me, and my sister suggests I drive off to find mixer.

To calm me.

Two corners away from parking, the old Cad goes down for the count.

The Triple A superhero takes his own sweet time arriving, then another long interregnum on diagnosis and yet even longer on repair. However he does mention Rex, how all 6–5 of him cruised town in white leather on a Harley until just recently.

Rex lifted the first barbells I ever saw, which makes him over eighty at least, a good three months of his eightieth year now spent bed-bound after T-boning on an unfortunate semi outside the Tumbleweed Bar on said bike, according to Triple A. But he's better, he's home, Triple A tells me.

The Tumbleweed Bar—was it sold? I ask to keep him talking.

He hasn't heard about the bar, and my telling him about the $4 gas I pumped last week in faraway Jersey he takes as my way of showing I make more than he does.

I drive off grateful. Hearing about Rex is a real welcome home. He used to count wild horses for the state from a plane and land that plane in our backyard to scare the stupid duck that hung around the birdbath. My mother drank with Rex at parties after everyone else had found their coats and she never minded the duck. The ruts his plane left on our half acre—his signature hello—still mar the yard. I park the car right up beside the fence to that yard where my mother has left the door to bang, and peek in the back picture window. There my mother sits, smiling into those ruts, her gash of teeth as she lifts her glass the only bright spot.

I decide to steal the silver.

My sister is getting it. She spent all p.m. yesterday polishing every piece as shiny as a gun. It isn't that I really want it. I want the making of trouble, an instinct in the time of travail. Rex was the one who taught me that trouble should be loud and bold if it is to be at all so I drop the car keys to the floor from a foot off the table, and take off my clothes. My disguise.

My mother can't see very well. She glances at me twice while I'm stuffing the silver into a green plastic garbage bag before she says, Rex?

I am all white leather, at least from her direction, though I am only half again as tall as he is even in recent memory, and of course female. No wonder he lifted those barbells.

Mother cries out, Oh, Rex, and she uses a tone nobody denies, least of all me.

I let her pat me on the shoulder.

I just locked my clothes in the car, I say.

She starts and then nods if this is just a simple mistaken identity, as if my nudity made the same sense as hers and his so many years ago at the end of a foyer, with me in twisted Dr. Dentons about to ask for water.

What was all that noise? she says, turning to her back window. Burglars?

The fish forks, I tell her, shivering.

I hate fish, she says.

For once I agree with her.

Rex jumped into our swimming pool completely dressed, holding an armful of lilacs. Dad laughed about it the next morning, cleaning the pool, making long sweeps with a machine that moved like a reptile.

My sister hasn't missed the silver yet. We eat on flatware like most homeowners, all her nice shiny silver replaced by a row of sticks tucked inside the dun cloths. She gestures with her flatware fork, talking about how Dad always meant to barbecue Spotty, how he ran around the pit with those skewers and how Spotty barked and barked and finally bit him when he poked him.

Dad deserved it, I say.

We turn to Mom who is pouring herself silly, who is pretending that the clear liquid in the glass is detergent, or anyway that's what she tells us. It will wash two loads for sure. Then she drinks it down.

It was another dog, she says after, touching her napkin to her lips.

I dial him and he answers. Rasp, rasp. Sweetheart, he says.

Do I sound like her that much? I say.

Ah, the older one, he says. I saw you in your altogether yesterday.

You promised no binoculars, I say.

Sorry about your dad, he says.

Thanks, I say. I appreciate that.

He had it coming to him, he did his time in the I.C.U. and he hated it.

You could say that, I say. I don't know that he did.

Don't live in the past, he says. Rasp, rasp. You might get to like it.

Rex once lay in my sister's bed and refused to get out until she punched him. Get up, she said. I need my sleep too.

Rex told her he was mattress testing and babysitting at the same time, he told our parents he was somebody they could always rely on and stayed with us while our parents went out to see shrinks. He would've commended me on how well I parked my parents' car, such a big boat in such a small driveway, if I had just kept talking.

He commended Dad.

My sister wasn't standing in that foyer so many years ago, just me. That's why she can't have the silver. She should have been there to tell me what I was seeing. I consider jamming the grinder with fork after fork, listening to the noise tear into my skull and be done with it. My sister is looking into the refrigerator now, exclaiming that we still have two more days of leftovers to eat.

Carbon-dated, I hope, I say. I propose we give the Cad a test and take it to a restaurant.

Rex is standing at the edge of our lot when we pull out, waving his crutches.

I could put poison in the birdfeeder, I say. But he's too old to reach.

She gets my gist but says I'm being unreasonable. Something that happened so long ago?

He got away with it, I say. Sweet and simple.

The next morning is one morning too many. I empty the silver back into its bag, a series of tremendous crashes. My sister comes running in like I'm denting it. Maybe I am. It's important to get air to it, the oxidation process you know, I say over the noise, letting her explain all about how the chemicals in silver play black havoc with any and all the air it gets.

Did Mom drive out last night to get Chivas? I say when she subsides. I thought I heard something.

We inspect the side of the garage. We don't disturb her in the car, snoring.

He could drive for her, I say. He could wear his leather and drive. It's what he's always wanted. It will be a fairy tale that ends in happiness.

Except for his accident, she says. Maybe now he's prone to crashes.

I call him anyway.

Sweetheart, he says. For you, I would drive around the world. Your mother? She had her chance.

Weatherproof

Every airplane in the airport lands late because of weather but not his, the plane he's changing to, the one he's running to catch, so many gates from the one he's left. Loping along the moving sidewalk, he moves more than 3-D, he goes time-warped, he'll catch that plane, it's Einstein's travel, time demented, and no tube goes detumescent at its gate, not his, no, it's still airlocked and open—but not this time.

Time. Time out. You're out. He sits, he stands, he gets back in line. The game is this: only the agent knows the rules, only the agent slips through that gate. Mere passengers are defeated by fate, their feet, and the weather.

The snow falls free. One man tears up his ticket and tosses it up into the air, his own blizzard. I'm just a number, he shouts. If they named the planes, the way they do ships, he says as he sits down next to him, it would make it more personal. Lucinda will be here in an hour, he says, so sorry, it would be like the plane's perm wasn't taking.

He moves.

His brother doesn't know where he is. Permanently hospitalized, he's now blue and pneumonic. Someone has just noticed the second, the blood workup returned and glanced through right after lunch and a quick smoke and stop at the john and a chat about the ballgame. No one hurries about the workup, he has given them such a hard time, pinching at people the way he does, especially the nurse and the two men it takes to hold him down. He himself is not such a big man but the pain makes him big, and pinch, pain nobody's figured out yet, the why nobody notices. No stools, written over and over on his chart, is a wonder. Or is it really written so often, is it skipped because the nurses can't keep track, don't want to keep track, because he pinches, his blue lobster fingers pinch because he can't talk?

He never could talk. There, and there, and there, in his brain, he could never do a lot of things.

His doctor arrives after the bloodwork's exclaimed over, rung for in response or rung because the nurses want any excuse to complain about the pinching fingers to someone who could inject a drug or order restraints. The doctor's own plane is late—later in the day, a vacation charter full of other doctors as single as himself, looking to get laid outside the bedridden corridors of work, will lift off, that is, it's a plane headed for a beach.

The doctor watches him breathe as if he were a fish thrown up on one of those beaches but does not stand too close, for he sees those hands clench. Bedside for him is arm's length. The doctor considers probing his ears and imagines their deep insides whorled in emptiness, with nothing where words are made, or thought.

His brother taught him to walk, moving his arms and legs with his mother two hours a day, forcing him to make some link to the brain with this moving, trained him mornings before walking to school, and then again on return. He didn't want to walk but had to.

He doesn't want to learn that one more thing, death, either. Not that he should learn, really, and not that the hospital will teach him anything else but pain, and no one learns from his pinching except to stay away.

His brother's not thinking about him, he rarely does since he left behind the long terrible chore of moving those arms and legs two hours a day to make him learn. He stands at the window of the airport facility—it's not even a building—and none of the planes coming and going so slowly through the slant driving snow promise to take him any closer or even farther from where he needs to go. Everyone says this is no one's fault other than the over-personified weather's, that mythic swirl that shifts the system no one's held accountable for.

He wonders at the gray blank wall of weather on the other side of the glass and the texture of his brother's brain—why not his own?—registers, it is that blank. His brother's alive in an institution somewhere, that much he knows, the one he was designed for, exercised for, that his mother cast him into, saying everybody over the age of twenty-one moves out if they move at all. He himself moves toward the counter, he leaves that view of gray.

We'll be happy to book you on the next flight, says someone behind the counter that the facility has in plethora but seldom staffs, or staffs lightly, her one-staff happiness supposed to suffuse the entire lounge so full of un-loungeable people. But there are no more planes, he reminds her. Please use the phone, patronize the hotel that perhaps the facility owns, she says. But he does not lift the phone that dials itself the way it could, all by itself.

He thinks a plane will fly.

His brother raves. He can't talk and in pain this not-talking sounds almost like the sounds another person would make in pain. He pinches instead. The nurses stand by, stand off. No one wants to do anything but have someone sign the forms. *Who will sign for him if?* is what they've been discussing all day, trying to contact someone. He's already blue, says one nurse, he's probably even more of a vegetable than before.

There are always degrees, says the head nurse.

Tomatoes or turnips? says another.

It's a job, resuscitating. The IVs go in, the chest gets beaten, the cables connected. Someone will have to pay for it, the state or whoever isn't here to sign for him. They'd rather not do it anyway, they'd rather go off and have a smoke.

It won't matter about the brain if he lives, the doctor decides. He orders rest instead of the procedure and does not press his belly for blockage the way he should because the man pinches, and his plane awaits.

He's only human. How much less is only? is what the nurse wonders after she leaves, her car keys mislaid for a minute.

The chaplain can't know what prayers the man prefers. He says them all and then gets social with the nurses: that's what he does best, to protect the patients. He knows the man's home is making cuts, it's looking for any excuse to rid itself of patients like him. He tries the phone of the brother listed but there's no answer. It's a luxury to have someone to sign, who belongs to you enough.

Every intestine in his system is plugged now, and turning to poison. He can't sit up, he can't. With animals, they're put on a shunt or get stabbed at some spot and the buildup releases quickly. By law, he is not an animal. The nurses say a man who pinches might bite. He fights when they strap on restraints.

His brother sits, stopped at the gate. Not even a toothbrush, is what he's realizing. And no one to call, if he could, not even on the self-calling phones—those lines are down too. The big gray storm still builds, the vast storm wall tightens around the facility, all the gray goes black but is it night? The thick cloud released from one of those rooms for people who can't quit is dark enough, or it could be all the exhaust of a century of plane-flying collected on one runway. Or fallout. He moves to sit in front of the TV bank that doesn't say anything local with its news and its reports on sports. He just sits there, stopped, until the attendant comes by with her cute ass and says, Are you still here? That plane left an hour ago.

Don't Look Now

I saw that film sitting under a tree in Sudan in the company of an Italian priest and the man I was with, she says.

She rearranges her legs, since that matters so much in a shrink's office. Dr. K is new, young—well, anyone's younger than she is—and, she presumes, has read all the books on the shelves behind him.

What am I forgetting? she says. Nicholas Roeg, he was the director. The most frightening film I've ever seen. Back then you would've seen it because everyone saw everything that came out as soon as possible, there were so few new films.

She lapses into silence to see if Dr. K will prompt her, or if he's one of those who will wait forever.

A long minute later he says: What was the film about?

A couple travels to Venice, she begins, because they are grieving the death of their daughter and the husband is restoring a church. They meet a clairvoyant who says their dead daughter is trying to warn them of danger. The film had the color of the pigeons that were always flying up, and red from the bad dwarf's cape.

Dr. K. isn't bothering to take notes, he will improvise. She stares at the papered-over window behind his head. The dwarf had a knife, she says. Inadvertently the husband becomes a suspect in a murder case. Cunnilingus was involved. Surely the priest was scandalized.

He smiles. She's taken aback: shrinks don't smile. She always tries to make them smile but most of the time they keep a straight face. But scandal is always amusing.

The man I was with made it a point to talk about the film and the sex, she says. The priest was handsome and friendly. I was embarrassed. Did I turn the embarrassment into fear? I was definitely afraid of the man I was traveling with, that he would turn on me.

She looks again into the opacity of the window but doesn't see it this time. I could hear the blood-sucking bats settling in the trees above us during the credits.

Very Graham Greene, says Dr. K.

That sounds like a compliment but she doesn't say so. Dr. K has gray eyes, not unfriendly, and needs a haircut.

The priest was so handsome, she says, even collared and wearing khakis. The collar must've been hot. I thought even then about what that symbolized with regard to sex, a choke collar. That decade was all about sex.

He scratches his nose. Bored already? Or uncomfortable with the topic?

The priest's English was as bad as my Italian, she says, not looking anywhere near Dr. K. The man I was with loved to pretend he could understand whatever language even if he didn't know a word of it. About the same age, the two of them enjoyed each other tremendously while piecing out the movie all over again in the dark of the night, long after the projector was packed away and the wind had died down. Especially that one scene.

She looks down at her hands. That part when the dead girl turns out to be the dwarf. Donald Sutherland was the lead.

What did you do while they were talking?

She finds the question taxing, surely a sign that it might lead somewhere she doesn't want to go. I had lunch with Donald once, she says, and visited a rare-book store with him, trying to get him to act as host to a project.

Did you succeed?

I did. I had just become a blonde and had blisters in my scalp from the bleach, and I had balls. I find that hard to imagine now.

Dr. K appears to be listening, but a little too intently. Is that what you want back? he says. That kind of imagination?

Well, she says. Sutherland never did the work.

He nods as if she's answered the question.

What I find hard to believe, she says, is that I have any memory at all of the monastery courtyard, of the Sudanese who came and went while the movie ran on. How few stopped to watch. I couldn't understand why they weren't riveted. Sure, it wasn't their language but nearly everyone in Khartoum spoke English or Arabic, along with six other languages. But why were we watching the film in a monastery?

Maybe the priest didn't know about that scene.

Unprecedented, a shrink offering an answer.

The priest ran the film series. He had a mission to fulfill, she says. Colonial conversion?

He observes the cockroaches dying on his wall, says the shrink. Gives them the last rites. Escape, that's what people do when they're out of their element.

I'm not talking about fate, am I? How we had to see that film in that context then.

The idea of fate isn't very useful in therapy, he says.

She nods, and waits for the wry expression on his face to return to professional.

The priest was funny, she says, and sad. He came from Naples and said in his terrible English that he was a spy before he signed up for time in the monastery, a spy in the Algerian war for the French. It was so twisted, he said, though no one would have said twisted then. He was doing penance in Sudan and had nearly forgotten why, teaching hordes of Sudanese girls in the high school. You see, I was listening. Maybe I listened like a shrink while the two of them talked. After all, whenever I said anything, the man I was with repeated my every word, and only then did the priest respond. There was no point in talking.

You were made invisible, says Dr. K.

Like you? But you have power. When you repeat what I say, you magnify it.

He nods slightly. The requisite tissue box sits on the far end of the bookshelf. She would have to get out of her seat to get one, or he would have to dispense one. More power.

I remember how the endless claustrophobic alleys of Venice in the movie quite captured the feeling of being lost as a tourist. I felt the full terror of that after we left Khartoum, of being unable to read the Venetian signs and getting irredeemably lost. The man I was traveling with often went on ahead. I was pregnant by then.

Dr. K. clears his throat. As I remember it, the film's about the psychology of grief and the effect the death of a child can have on a relationship.

You did see it?

Yes. I remembered it when you mentioned the claustrophobia.

Mistaking the dwarf with the knife for a child, that's what really undid me. A sort of precursor to my son's death. An accident, she says, not due to a murdering dwarf.

I see, says Dr. K.

Nobody does. She looks at her hands again because there they are, sitting in her lap. The film was about how nobody understood each other, nobody understands what it's like to lose a child. The horror.

She can't tell the shrink that all she wanted to do was have sex after the child died, just the way the couple did in the film, or he'd think she was trying to seduce him, and drop her. But isn't a shrink like any audience, and you have to seduce them a bit to make him listen? I remember the guns in the Sudanese museum we visited the next day, she says, stacked up so gaily, celebrating the vanquished, their ammunition, their tanks, all the photographs of the dead.

Dr. K. pulls his hands out from under his desk. They begin to move to signal their session is finished, move like an Italian's, with eloquence. Or does she just imagine the nationality of his raised palms?

Next week.

She plunges into the snow of New York that has piled up during her session, taking care to follow the footprints others have left before her. Do they all go in and never come out? Across the street is Madison Square Park and dogs chase after balls despite the snow, their leashes and their owners trailing after them.

She hadn't heeded the film's warning, she should have resisted the man she was with that night and never gotten pregnant. And to have been so lost in Venice—at every turn she faced another baffling decision. She remembers how the priest couldn't quit talking about the movie afterward, how he had called out the title as they were leaving: *Don't Look Now*.

But she has to.

Fortuneteller

How can this Indian guy know anything?

My friend nurses, her wet pink nipple popped out, popped in. It's the East, she says, and turns up the raga she's playing. This mystic is the best.

The raga doesn't drone loud enough to drown out my baby's cries. Okay, he's not a baby, he's almost two and says so with a digit on one hand and his thumb on the other—and he's crying for milk, any milk, inspired by the two-year-old ecstasy of his milk brother's toes writhing in pleasure. I hand him a sippy cup. Long ago she nursed mine and hers and that's his beef. Now we were going to be business sisters. We'd just come back from the garment district to check prices on how much it would cost to manufacture baby slings like the ones I'd seen in Africa but with an adjustable buckle. Except that the guy in the office laughed at us and our firstborns, even hers, with his rabbi-fixed face.

Her hands free—her boy can help himself—she lights some incense. Credit is like the future, she says through its haze. We need more of it.

Pre-baby, she hung a tanka in her bedroom and shared jobs and the names of Chinese medicinal plants I ought to be stewing. Not exactly by osmosis I learned and overheard that eastern tendencies bested our beliefs, that Baby Buddha invented laughter and what did we invent? Horror. An Indian soothsayer of Hindu persuasion, at least a sidekick of Buddhism, ought to be worth the long subway ride. He would tell us our real futures.

We pack the sippy cup but no diapers—everybody is past that—for the trip on the train is long and thirsty. Trees and a swingset and squirrels at the end, a park-walk, it is the promise of expedition that the boys gentle at, they stop kicking and arching their backs with their stroller incarceration and glare at each other.

But we are late. The line is so long we can't see the front of it, just the steps up into the place that is strictly for students of theology, the study of god, a practice almost eastern to me, a fallen-away Catholic, so fallen the future is only fiery, or so says the pigtailed man in front of us, crossing himself. I know I'm not going to get much of a break in this future—it's my friend's boyfriend's boy in that stroller, born to me out of a confusion of rooms late at night that remained uncorrected just long enough. The boyfriend had such a Christ-fear approaching his thirty-third birthday that the spewing of seed seemed to him his best chance for immortality. His boy is so happy, not fearful at all. Despite his nostalgia for the nipple, his cheer has already attracted a true suitor with whom I am sending out invitations next week for a ceremony.

My friend holds no grudge about the mixup of bedrooms, he wasn't her type. Her baby's father actually is a rabbi, another aspect of the Buddha, she says, only closer to her own ancestral roots. Married? Yes, with ten of his own, safe from any baggage, she says, in the obedience department. But now she is searching for a more occidental connection that maybe this Indian guy has a bead on.

We inch forward, the kids tethered or chased, the rest of the line reflecting their impatience with meditative stances, holier-than-thou resignation, then the kids fall asleep in their strollers, and then she goes first.

She must have heard what she wanted to hear, she looks so pleased after having her hand read, pleased into a big smile, and the guy, business-suited but turbaned, agrees to read her son's hand as a bonus, and does so, telling her about future musical ability and artistic tendencies, which, if she were a sensible mother, should scare her to death.

My turn next, me at the very end of this very long line, and he looks at my hand and his Hindu face fades. He says there is strife and sadness and nothing much good in it, that's what I hear or rather he says very little, which, as any polite person knows, means you say what you can about what is good and leave out the rest. Still wanting the reading to be worth all the waiting, I say, what about reading my son's?

The reader unclasps my son from his toy drumstick, spreads his little star of a hand in his own, and the boy stirs out of sleep. The Indian guy, said to be so certain and accurate about all of his prophecies, stares at it and then closes it.

The life line is too short, he says.

My friend who is jiggling her rabbi son says, What?

I don't answer, I quick-check my boy's harness and whip him down that short set of stairs fast, I thank the Indian guy with my back turned, carefully bumping us toward the subway, and my friend, after a minute, bumps after me.

He was right by the end of the year, when all I wanted was wrong.

The Cloud Painter's Lover

The orange car the sixteen-year-old has been eyeing ever since it pulled in front of them miles and miles ago is sucking up the air—can't they feel it? The boy lunges at the windshield, he smacks the windshield so hard with his fist, with his *Open the window!*, that it shatters. She grabs the wheel from the backseat so his father can get the kid calmed down, then it's hell while the father wrenches the car off the freeway, chunks of bloodied windshield flying everywhere, the roar of traffic after the big *pow* of explosion.

She takes over driving, she weeps at emergency while the father hauls out the kid who won't go, won't go, and then the kid bolts inside, six feet of mania. He's his father's size, he's got his big frame, his big hands, but his father's are shaking, he can't get open the door as fast as his son. He gallops after him toward the emergency entrance where orderlies or whatever the hell you call them come out the door toward him in squadron formation, the boy caught in their arms, struggling.

I don't bite! his son screams and his father nods while they jab the needle into the boy's arm, the cold drug flowing, he nods with big cartoon eyes.

On the way home, she says he was right about the windshield. The air feels great.

Ha. His father isn't steady yet so his Ha is barked but he agrees, he too likes the air rushing at them as if they had a convertible instead of this wreck, but not the gravelly feel of the broken glass bits on the seat, whatever they couldn't get brushed out.

She puts her hand on his arm, the one on the wheel. We could eat, she says, nodding sharp at the drugged kid in the back. He's not going to wake up for a while.

I can't figure out what time of night it is, he says. I think it's yesterday. Isn't it yesterday? The other boy's still out? When did he say he was coming home?

The window screen rips.

I fixed that, his father gasps straight from sleep.

Count backwards, she says.

A kitchen thing falls.

He sits up, he heaves his legs over the side of the bed, head still bowed.

At least he's home, she says. At least the other one's asleep.

Fuck, says the boy in the hall, says in his not-at-all-tired voice, the wired one.

His father whacks the door into the wall, grips the kid vomiting on his feet, just grips him.

She's afraid to look, afraid this one's sick too. Are you sick? she calls from the bed.

Saliva trailing, the kid smiles big at the door. I tried crack, he says.

Give her a man in a ripped t-shirt with a loud motorcycle or matted hair to the shoulders, a flip way with a cigarette—her lover has all those traits and more. Of course, in her day, when bad boys were bad boys, they never had parents—or anyway, none you ever saw. Ten years after they met, he turned parent by proxy by adopting his dead brother's two boys because their mother was too much of a drunk to manage them. The little boys called him Daddy right away—so endearing. He surprised her by taking on the role so easily, calling time-out, reading them stories, buying the boys squirt guns and ice cream.

He surprised her again when, two years later, she saw a document she shouldn't have, two whole years later. At the time they were 10,000 miles out of L.A., on an island that was building a huge casino that needed clouds, his kind of big-money, low-art job. They had been dressing for its opening at the time, a tux for him, a formal handsewn from Singapore for her, when she found the document searching for a pair of pearls in the last drawer of the house. Read fast, unreadable, she tucked it into her clutch. She was in shock already from the boys asking her about cunnilingus an hour before, no—told her how it was done, courtesy of the last summer spent with their mother.

His wife.

It was an accident, he told her at the end of the party. He was helping his brother build a house a state away, you remember? and she was hanging around. His brother was just helping him out, living with her, a woman she knew nothing about.

Two accidents? she said.

He bowed, on bended tux knee, asking her to forgive him. Other partygoers assumed he was proposing and clapped.

She didn't have the money to fly home so they worked it out beneath the fake sky full of his clouds, over the slot machines and a fountain of alcohol neither of them much cared for. Was she going to bear children at the age that they had met? No. He had wanted a family.

Wanted. She brushes her teeth, turning the word over in her brain like a ball you could throw and hit someone with. Past tense.

Now he's asleep where he landed after locking the crack-tester into his room. The gray couch sets off his paleness, his white hair punk-straight off his head, his still handsome face pinched even in sleep. He has heart problems, Mr. Gruff Sex and Long Kisses, Mr. That's Art with a Capital A, and eyebrows that stay peaked. Heart problems! He hasn't slept through the night since the boys were "adopted" so long ago, with those fake papers he waved at her while saying how much he loved her. Society, after all, is artificial, he said in defense, its rules dreamed up just for order. If you fall out of step, is it a crime? Children per se are not inherently bad, they come and here they are.

Though she could no longer make those cheerful art videos like *How to Fry a Grapefruit* that museums appreciated and collected, she had given up on being angry. She had taken a job of subbing at the boys' school so she could keep a cheerful eye on them but her job soon became more about the money. Fewer clouds on the horizon. Last month the administration required her class to write a thank-you note to a much-hated principal. The kids refused. She suggested they write about their real feelings and then put that paper aside and write something phony. One child complained to his mother.

Without the subbing job, she had no idea that the younger one, as blond and thin as a Pop-Tart, had skateboarded into the wrong crowd. These guys are all about the exercise, he smoke-screened, they don't even like computer games. What they liked, apparently, was crack. So bright he tested out of his grade and so bad he flunked it twice and had to be homeschooled, he was so damaged he couldn't talk during the first six sessions of therapy.

He worries when his father skips a meal, he gives him his share. Now he's banging something loud against his bedroom wall.

She'd planned to visit a graffiti show today that she would never take the boys to, too much glorification of the "writers," as these destroyers of public surfaces are called by the adoring newspapers. The show is supposed to be so hip, so totally gang-positive. Adolescents—black and white—have it tough enough here without gang influence, positive or negative. Last week six neighborhood boys hung around the park ten minutes after the movie let out and a police helicopter and sixteen patrol cars descended, weapons first. Curfew, they bull-horned. The boys scattered. Big mistake. One of the boys was heat-sensed out of a compost bin. On the day of the hearing, all of the fathers had to take off work, but the cops didn't bother to show, the judge just collected the fines.

The older boy slugs his father *Good morning*, right where he hit his arm falling off a ladder at work. The old man yelps. The boy responds by belching, his head inside the fridge. They sometimes work together and he's good, he wears himself out. Sloe-eyed like his father, his chest broadening, *Cute* is his tag. He tells girls he and his dad paint clouds. Lie down, he tells them. I'll show you how—and forgets to go back to class. His hooky-playing is supposed to be made up this week but he's staying home to get over the drugs the hospital put into him the night before, making his moves zombie and tired, a little like his dad's. His younger brother's not going anywhere either, today he's utterly useless, cracked, unable to stand upright. She has to keep them both home and good luck, says her lover on his way to work, taking the keys of the car that still has a windshield.

So much for the graffiti exhibit.

She is tired. They aren't her kids. She sits on the couch and pets her dog. When the dog howls at a passing car, she determines he hasn't been fed. Someone would've had to open a new bag of food. She opens it. Half of the wet food in the can inside the fridge is gone. The younger boy likes it, desperate from their new routine of locking the cupboards so the boys won't sell food for drugs. Of course neither has an allowance. The very word.

Put us in a foster home, they insist. Just not with Mom.

Mom keeps boyfriends who shoot and boyfriends who shoot up. She used to be a nanny until she and her employer got drunk while the boys and her charge set fire to the backyard. Now she is born again in a huge church not far from where she cooks for a living, a church the boys are required to attend. They roam the church grounds with other kids, doing "youth activities," activities that girls fear, that girls tell on, that girls cooperate with.

Stop says the sign, their father says. Nobody's going to make you but you'd better think about it.

There are good boys. The school has examples, boys who blush and boys who save up for Mother's Day. She has talked to scout leaders and not the preying type her boys insist they are, and she has even seen actual altar boys at work. Forget that, the boys say, that's really dangerous. Their friends invade their place every few days, crash the keys of the piano and then set up beer pong on its lid, telling her it's urine in the paper cups, not to worry.

Mental illness, she tells the younger one about his brother's problems, but last week when the older one came home with cigarette burns up his arm, the younger picked out a face on the flesh between his forefinger and thumb and kept it raw by rubbing it with an eraser. Something's still crashing in the bedroom. Over and over, a percussion recital just for her. No—she looks at herself in the mirror, mouth twisting—not for her, it's not personal. She pries open the lock to the door with a knife. The skateboard is attached to a spring to make it bounce forever against the very battered wall, and the boy has escaped through another ripped screen.

She puts the leash on the dog who needs walking anyway, she will find that boy and set him straight, now and not later. At the door, she tells the older one, Yes, he can use her computer—for history, not pornography.

What's the difference? he yells.

She passes the geranium pots of the complex, she walks toward the beach a mile away. All the ozone will perk her up and the smog is moot, the dog at least amenable. She walks and tries not to think.

She fails. He says he doesn't want to trap her in marriage, or she'll be legally responsible for them too.

And if you were carted off to the hospital, she says, I wouldn't be allowed to see you, and your sons will tell them not to resuscitate you.

He laughs. Don't give them any ideas. Just think—you'll get more social security from your first husband if we don't get married.

True, but not much of a reason for him to stay married to that—

No—she isn't angry, she's furious. His head's in the clouds, she says to the shrink, even to the social worker you get when the rules get out of control, even the rules. Her lover is an airhead. But she knows he sees over the clouds to some clear space she wants to be in too, and she doesn't leave.

The suburbs stretch as far as the eye can see, hill and dale. She spent a good fifteen years single in them, she knows them well. A dog park lies south, a closer goal than the beach. She shoots the curve of the subdivision she's passing with her iPhone, all the camera she has for her cheerful art that the boys haven't stolen and hocked. She keeps the phone under her pillow at night. It's in our house, they say. Whatever's in it is ours.

House, not home.

She walks on, creating a suite of stills: red blooms against the blue-painted patio, the face of a vendor asleep beside his Hot Tamales, and every license plate she can find at every angle, a series that ends on the face of the younger boy standing on top of the hill, his board under his feet, his hands empty, such a long face.

She can't see past him over the hill and then she does, she sees blood streaming from the head of another boy lying on the curb next to a splintered skateboard. A car is stopped midstreet and a bald guy is standing beside it, not walking toward the boy but holding out his phone. Sirens scream faint in the distance.

A friend? she says.

The younger one gets off his board and puts it under his arm. Fuck, he says.

She takes his hand as if he were a kid.

The party's on a lawn where the houses all around it shout Deco-Deco, and tiny bits of protein presented on planes of starch are passed by college students dressed very much like caterers. He shakes the hands of the art-illustrious, the ones covered in lustre, he tells her later, and lustre she guesses is a finish hard to wash off. They all know him, she is proud to see, he has a place amongst them that makes him want to leave early, before they can get him into compromising positions, is what he says after, but she makes him stay longer and grovel, he says, until he shuts them all up by showing him pictures of his boys. Now she says, Look at the sun, which is showing up already at the very edge of the ocean you seldom notice even though it is so close, the ocean snapping at the sand where they sit.

Another dawn but a good dawn. No clouds.

Crickets call from the boys' lizard's cage inside, the calls fewer and fewer, more and more panicked. She's crocheting squares, white patch, brown, in a chair in the yard amongst the few wisps of grass she's plucked dandelion-free. Two windowless sheds stay empty and locked behind her, extra space for the boys to do what in? Too hard to monitor. It's good the older boy kicked out the door to his bedroom, she doesn't even have to open it to see what he's up to. At least all the writing he's encircled the room with is painted over. They had to take him to emergency again and at last his mother admitted that her mother went out of control too. Not her, of course. The younger boy's door is gaffer-taped together. He wants a door no matter what. He's afraid of his brother now, he cries at therapy. Both boys now recline in their rooms with their devices, silent, so silent she goes outside to worry and crochet squares in this small square of grass.

The boys' father appears and stations himself at the threshold of the backyard, neither in nor out, holding a bowl of cereal. Someone left teethmarks in the butter, he says.

Cut the teeth part off, she says. She watches her fingers keep to the crochet pattern. Butter is expensive.

I didn't do it, says the older boy who pushes at his father from behind and shows him his teeth. He holds two chicks in his hands, one black, one yellow.

Are you going to feed them to the dog? she asks.

Dogs don't like chickens, cats do. He bought them, he says about his father.

Two-fifty apiece, his father says. They're soft.

They like to eat gravel, says the boy. He sets them down and leaves them to peck at the little grass at her feet. The dog sniffs them, sits on his haunches in boredom.

His father spoons into his cereal. I'm going to take the boys on a hike, he says at the bottom of the bowl. Want to come?

They'll wear shoes?

He laughs as if he's not sure.

She whips a finished square off the needles. I'll bring the water.

They are standing in the shade of a rock with the dog, the younger boy jumping up and down in the distance, the older one spread out on top of the rock, lighting matches and dropping them onto the desert floor.

See that cloud, says the father. Turner painted it with yellow, blue, ivory, and pink. That's how you get a good cloud.

The dog barks at one of the matches falling too close. The boy squints at another flame in his hand.

I'll bet you don't know he used to be head of the art department at the university, she says, stepping into the sun to avoid a match.

You went to school? says the boy.

Vietnam made you want to go to school. His father puts out the match with his foot.

The younger brother hops toward them. She squats to look at the cactus spine in his shin. He does not cry, he just sticks his leg out at her.

You're a failure, says his older brother to his father.

Seriously? asks his father, so calm it's as if the heat of the desert has baked his emotions solid.

She pulls out the spine and the younger one doesn't scream, he wrenches the spine out of her hand and threatens his brother with it. His brother leans over the edge of the rock with a new burning match. Money, money, money, he says to his dad. That's the point. Not art.

Let's go, the younger one says, swiveling away. He pretends to skateboard over the rough sand, his leg wound forgotten. Let's get out of here.

If we go now, she says, we'll be stuck in school traffic.

Stuck in school, stuck in school, chants the younger boy, hopping away. That would be the worst.

His father throws a rock into the distant desert horizon. What would make you a success? he asks the older boy.

He's gained weight since he's been on medication. A lot of girls, he says.

I had that, says his father.

She's about to say something—isn't she supposed to?—when the dog pulls hard on his leash. She wants to let him go and find whatever jackrabbit he thinks is out there, she doesn't want to be tethered to him too. But after she says, Don't pull, he doesn't, he listens to her.

The younger one says the car is too far away, couldn't somebody drive over here and pick them up?

She remembers then she left the iPhone behind with the bottle of water no one wanted, she walks the ten feet back to the car and locates it. Commemorative moment, she announces on her return to the rock. I want all three of you to jump as high as you can together—when I say *Jump*.

No, says the older boy but he slides off the rock anyway, breaking his fall with his cigarette-burned arm, landing at their feet.

Jump! she says. To her surprise, all three of them—the wizened white-headed lover, the filled-out older boy, the lanky younger one—throw themselves into the air, each of them with a smile jerked onto their face by the falling part of the motion, all their six feet each an inch off the desert floor, and down.

The younger one keeps on jumping all the way to the car.

Money is the point? she says, getting behind the driver's seat, behind its new windshield. Say that when you're standing there, rich and unhappy and alone.

You believe all that stuff the media tells you? says the older boy, throwing himself into the back seat.

Yeah, you're so gullible, says the younger one, and manufactures a loud noise with his armpit and hand.

Apropos of a look between her and his father, the older one says: You think I'm stupid? You'll see—I'm going to college.

The younger one stops his noise, he stops and stares out the window. In the rearview mirror she sees his face go cold and set.

You're smart too, she says, and she doesn't regret it.

Motherliness

The car slides and hits. Maybe due to leaves blown over rain-slick, maybe a tire let-go but, yes, a body goes down.

You would think doom would settle, that people would flee a street so wet and blood-jetting, but they toe the curb, dialing disaster, disaster, picturing it with their phones, at least three of them, while the car drives away. A flinch or a swerve and it leaves, pavement-happy, so fast the phones are still being fumbled free in a rain as dark as the letters and numbers of the car's tail end.

So far nothing too unusual. The rain smears the blood, the left person doesn't rise, brush the front of a torn sleeve, or sneeze from the effort. The by-now chorus of wet bystanders doesn't talk except for short bits: *You did? I can't reach. Throw me a line,* the last having to do with a pocketful of cord one man tries to tie off the blood with, and then his belt. Others have reached professionals, yes, they have, and stand in the rain debating exit, looking askance, which is elsewhere. Don't move the victim, they call out before they turn away into the dark. Few get close enough to know if anything is moved, then they move.

There's lightning, and other cars, there's a wailing no one wants to hear, people who look at other people for permission to witness what they can't look away from. But it's someone calling for Mother, you can hear the faintest mutter from that someone at last doing something other than bleeding.

And still it keeps raining, says the man sans slicker who bends down to see if he can hold the hand of the downed person and succeeds, him crouched while the others begin to—is the word evaporate?—change from the state of stilled attention to wallpaper, then gone. The ambulance slams out its gurney to a scene so deserted it looks as if the hand-holder caused the injury.

The car had Mother in it, says the injured to the man. She did it.

The hand-holder is so shocked she's even talking that what she says doesn't register fast enough for a What? The medics are tucking her, are taking stock, are inputting vitals. Mother, says the injured one. At the wheel.

Name? asks the head medic of the hand-holder as if he were an intimate, had been holding that hand before the accident.

I'm nobody to her, he says.

The back of the ambulance slams shut as the medic takes note.

There's a party to go to, people are peeling off their outer garments for showing off inner, and hanging the peeled outside the door on hangers. He doesn't leave his coat, he needs an extra layer over himself until he can swallow and coat his insides with beer or wine, those forgetters. In front of him, a girl, judging from the chewed nails adjusting her headband, talks about her mother with such urgency he stops three steps in. A girl with big breasts and her own motherliness, tipsy.

I was just on the street, he begins.

The music blares and quiets, then blares again.

I'm not on the street anymore, she says but she's teasing, he guesses she's never been homeless, she's never been pimped or run over, chewed nails or not.

There's no point in injecting pathos when parties portend so much otherwise. He tries confusion. Your mother is discreet?

I'd never say that, she says.

She can can-can, she shows him. I need a wider skirt, she says, flailing her arms to one side or the other. My mother taught me.

He still hasn't taken off his coat. He is slumped in a soft chair that the hostess has just left, and balances his newly fetched drink on his belt buckle. Her legs kicked this way remind him of the body flung up after the car hit, how the shoes went high into the rain then fell with it. It wasn't a body then, but a woman.

Has the rain stopped? he says, finding her parka an hour later.

She's staring at her phone where such information flashes. She does not say No, she has not said No all night. He is counting on her not to say it.

They step out into the wet night a few blocks from the scene he'd held hands in, they step out and the night makes the accident not matter at all, though he does hesitate at the corner where the cars thicken, an artery that crosses that block, they even walk past where the ambulance turned itself around, where he's tempted to tell her but then not, letting the light change, and their conversation flop from one nervous observation to the next.

In his room, because hers is still crammed to the roof with divorce stuff, she says, he watches headlights cross the ceiling. She has nestled into the corner made by his arm crook and side and now makes another snore similar to the one that had surprised him awake: sniffle in, snort out. In his awake state, he considers: Why did the dying woman or at least the badly injured woman hold her mother responsible? Her tone sounded pleading more than accusatory. Had the mother really been at the wheel? His memory shreds the sequence to bits that make sense by themselves but are not quite coherent. Isn't that how you sound after trauma?

His or hers?

She was so certain.

He rises and, feeling suddenly modest in the moonlight, hitches a towel around his waist and pulls on a sweater. The refrigerator holds nothing consoling.

They say nice things to each other at daylight. They could gather mushrooms, she says, adjusting her headband as if it's receiving messages from elsewhere.

Does it? he wonders after saying that he could use a walk.

While they ply the thick leaves around the base of the so many trees that the meadow ends in, her eyes flick from the ground to his crotch, he can almost feel her inspection. Not unpleasant. She says, my mother's left sixty messages in the past two days.

He nods, then denies the mushroom at their feet could be good. I don't think so. They bruise blue.

She insists.

They take the bus back, a bag of what they've collected at their feet between them, like some executed pet, but with a danger that lurks. His decision not to tell her about the night before unites them, the unspoken knits their exchanges in parentheses neither can quite work out. It's attractive, this mystery. How long can the long lashes of rain keep this going? They stripe at the bus window without the least concern.

He holds her hand.

Mexican Honeymoon

Dogs tap their toenails beneath the staircase in the courtyard. He flaps his napkin at one, *Caffay o-lay!*, ordering in sight of the half-ruined pyramids, *O-lay*, and the dog shows his teeth, that dog tears off a piece of the napkin, which relaxes the dog—he stops barking—making him happy the way he, the man, is happy with what's left of his honeymoon.

But she is uninterested. Everyone else watches them or pretends not to, every faux honeymooning bureaucrat and bureaucrat's mate who will never receive a real proposal, not that kind here. All of them are secretly married to someone else—that's how little they know each other, it's where Mexicans go for this, even the bellhop says so. They like the man teasing the dog. It's what they're all doing, the little explorations of the not married, the sly poking of the adulterers.

But the woman with the man could've been a man, she is so uninterested, a man would've been more interested. The crows, however, are interested after his *O-lay* napkin flap, the crows come for the crumbs she's made of her toast, falling, then winging high just before landing at their unshaded table. She could be one of those crows—the red-black of her hair and her intense focus on the nauseous-making crumbs instead of him, but inside her roils me. I've forgotten slamming into being but here I am, just a cell or two or three inside her womb, I'm what's making the toast nauseating, piquing her disinterest, brightening the bright late morning sun on the table.

His flapping subsides. He pats the dog, sleek with tourist leavings, while two waiters balance and cart plates and saucers, empty or not, off their table. A cloud hovers, a hiatus in her mood that allows him to turn to her just as the mariachi band, out all night, clatters and slumps into the adjacent chairs. Before he can make any further effort, one of them strums, brushes his hand automatically or accidentally against his strings, and of course the crew sings. They can't help themselves, it's an aubade, the sad morning after, it's the song I'm in, wriggling inside her, with the cafe au lait, con leche, con lechery my father would say years later to my by-then permanently indifferent and hence irresistible mother.

Listening to the music, the couples, errant or not, drink from their cups without looking at each other. My father searches his pockets, making the music of change in chorus, the music of never enough change, while the strummer, his gold-braided-sweat-mooned uniform dazzling the crows and perhaps the crowd when he stands, sways as he sings as if drunk but no drunk could sing so sadly at this hour after singing so long. It is as if he too has spent the night in the little bright blue and yellow room under the gorgeous staircase until 2 a.m. when my father abducted his new wife, coaxed her up to the roof to look at the stars, and found instead the night overcast and bee boxes with queens about to fly. At night, screamed my father into their dolorous buzzing, even at night? Whereupon my mother, bold in her cameo-colored nudity, leaned out over the roof to avoid the bees, and vomited.

I had been lodged inside her mere minutes.

The adulterers and the newlyweds and the fornicators sigh, then they pay for the band's breakfast and probably lunch. Even my father abandons his coin search and stuffs five of his peso notes into the upturned hat of the still strumming singer.

Afterward, my mother and father go horseback riding into the basalt canyons to further distract themselves from each other, to enjoy a few moments without carnal rawness. I remember—I hate horses today, the heaving, the lather. The large bay my father rides knows right away he needs to flee from this new indifferent wife and races straight for the rocks. My mother screams, and her horse takes off into the opposite canyon. Their guide thoughtfully turns his horse after my mother instead of my father and finds her weeping at a spring not far away, her dark hair not unattractively framing her wet face, and her horse pawing and shuffling, reins down, not even really wanting the water.

Senorita, he says because he calls all women that, it is hotel policy, and then he says a lot of other things in Spanish.

It is I who made her dismount and throw herself into his arms. That's what she tells my father when he rides in, his horse cowed by his rider's *O-lay* bravery, his horse having stopped short at the rocks in hopes that his rider will catapult over him but he didn't, he had his legs clamped tight.

My stomach is upset, that is all, she says, that's why we're embracing like that, in the basalt canyon so dark and shiny.

What my father doesn't know is how to dismount from the wild ride his bride is about to give him for years, propelled by me, always me, first inside her honeymooning like some ride-along bee and then not, however present *in extremis* after the return home and subsequent wait. Even still. To wit, at this juncture, the basalt canyon grinning down at all of us so puny in the landscape or so dramatically framed, the rented horses backdrop and catalyst, my mother's crying on the guide's shoulder confuses the guide. He is years younger than my father, a boy really, and he shoves her away, forgetting his salaried hotel indifference and his manners, the feigned cheerfulness. My father flies at him, furious not only that he has caught her in his arms, in the wiles of her cameo-skin and black Irish, not Mexican, thick hair, but also, yes, because of her indifference, and he and the guide exchange blows, both of their blows glancing off because that's how it is in real life, glancing or so solid you don't talk about it later.

Later she lays her clothes in her suitcase. It is how she lays them, so smoothly, and flattened with the heel of her hand, that doesn't suggest packing, it's a slowness that belies leaving, even a sorrow. Not indifference.

He doesn't notice.

He stands at the single window of their understairs hotel room, long and bare of shades, open to the courtyard, and watches the waiters push chairs into rows for something the two of them won't see. There is so much they won't see and he feels that and brushes it away quick like those bees that night, and turns back to her, so radiant with me inside. He asks her the way you would, struck by the ineffable, if she has change for the taxi, which she wordlessly fetches, which she presses into his hand, then kisses his cheek, bruised from the guide's glancing blow, kisses it so hard it stings.

He is silent. A hurt for a hurt. He folds the money into his pocket and picks up her suitcase, then his.

The Oscars

Her husband goes hard on her. No blushes—he goes hard all over, not just in the assumed area. He could have *Blip!* disappeared instead, how would his wife have liked that? He has to make a choice, his captors are waiting, they don't have time, that is to say, he says later, they didn't have enough time to cover the hole they'd made in time to get what they needed, so they make him go hard.

TV-entranced, he seems when his wife first notices, although he could have been going hard for some time, is what everybody says later. Watching TV he did in spades, true enough, but for professional purposes. He acted for a livelihood, which is why his wife thinks he is just Samuel Becketting her, standing there in the act of turning it on or off, standing so still in front of it when he could have been reading lines or going to the fridge.

He goes hard with his hand out.

He says they didn't mistreat him, that all he had to do was stand in the middle of a kind of stage and eat things he doesn't much care for—the food tasted like the cooking he does for himself while his wife tears down sets, her contribution to the theatrical arts. He ate the bland things they offered rather well, he knew that, and they took notes.

But of course his telling all this is later, after all that hardness has worn off, which takes months. At first his wife tries to soften his upraised hand by shaking it. The hand doesn't shake. She tries kissing his rocky lips, which only makes her cry. She then slaps his cheeks until they hurt her hand. He barely blinks. Finally she rubs her breast against that outstretched hand. His cock remains as stiff as his stiff thigh.

Their doctor, an avid fan, makes a house call. He wants to be an actor himself and considers this anomaly a private performance and, after checking his patient's perfectly beating heart, suggests she charge French intellectuals pay-per-view, and to be sure to videotape him for an art performance. This isn't a *Rain Man* thing or an *Awakening*, he says, but I will do endorsements if you need me to. Then he tells her a joke about a pope going into a pharmacy for a prescription that is so bad she throws him out.

She puts her husband at the window to get some sun. Voiceover work had been depressing him. He had been telling her how he could not stand it anymore when she called out to him from the kitchen to just go to the window, this sun is as close to a Florida vacation as he will get.

Standing in that sun, he begins to sweat and smell. She drags him back into a corner and dusts him occasionally. When their son visits, they wedge him into the bath for a scrubbing. Her son can't resist telling him a thing or two, his patriarchal stiffness making it so hard to clean his withers. Soon the son is angrier than he thought and his mother has to shush him, fearing his father might have heart failure, she says, instead of movement.

They invite his friends over. Perhaps the sound of all that competition will bring him around. But there is nothing worse than a stony audience. Their guests eat handfuls of trash party food, snap their fingers in front of his face and go home happy, escaping with *Not me* all over their faces.

The doctor performs clumsy magic tricks dressed in several yards of Christmas tree skirting. When the wife and the patient don't respond, he says, Pain, push a pin through his finger, light a match under his nose.

I read his reviews out loud, she says. That should have done it.

I'll bring my crystal ball, says the doctor. I'll summon the spirits. Bring him back to life.

Isn't that a little unethical for a physician? she says, into her third drink.

He laughs, and is quick to admire the cornstarch she sprinkles around his feet to mark if he moves when she isn't around.

It isn't a week later when he housecalls yet again. The crystal ball comes in a miniature bowling bag. He sets it up on top of a cloth-covered card table, and they both see her husband inside it, looking at his feet and eating things.

Give me a break, says his wife. He could do that at home.

She doesn't worry so much about him after that, at least not about how little food she manages to force down his hard throat. The doctor, however, begins to visit more often, in order to inject him with vitamins. He should stay in familiar surroundings, says the doctor, not the hospital. He tells his jokes sometimes so quietly she has to move closer for the punchline.

These jokes are always not funny, that is to say, they are laughable. Usually he improvises badly, with telling clauses omitted or bits foregrounded meant to be mere color, or else he memorizes from websites that belong to no one who has ever told a joke. She laughs anyway, they lighten her husband's hardness.

The doctor rarely arouses an audience. He makes a swine of himself, does comic things with fruit.

She becomes hysterical.

He's not exactly watching, he says, moving one of the bananas.

He might come around, she says.

We could try being very passionate for purely medicinal purposes, he says, mumbling into her collarbone.

For a hard case, she says.

Meanwhile, those who have him in captivity can now convincingly chew and amuse each other with long chewing performances based on his. They put into his upraised hand the object every actor wants, an award gilt and subhuman in form, eyeless and featureless, very much depicting themselves—a senseless race—and he softens.

The doctor and his wife happen to be writhing their way to the bedroom when he rubs his sore arm back to life, extricates himself from the umbrellas and comic hats of the closet he has been shoved into in a pique of their passion, and, shaking his head as if to clear his ears of odd noises, he heads for the fridge, feeling peckish. Otherwise, he feels extremely satisfied, a synthetic response to holding and having and, indeed, being among the Oscars. He is halfway through a bout of sandwich-making when his wife, hair wild, rustles into the kitchen.

I'm late, she says, stuffing her blouse into place; the set is not yet struck. She takes the sandwich from him and bites into it, an uxorial gesture meant to allay suspicion.

Time stands still for you, dear, he says.

Perhaps, she says, and she insists he follow her to work.

But I haven't showered, he says, sniffing himself.

She smiles at his bent head. You can't go into the bathroom, she says. It's broken.

Of course it could have been all programmed into your memory, she says, and something else happened entirely. Or else nothing happened at all, which is what you might suspect of anyone standing in front of a TV.

What do you remember of what people around you said while you were "gone?" asks the doctor, dropping by a few minutes later.

He says the reception was fuzzy, he could hardly hear in either place, what with all the hardness setting in.

He does not, however, pay the doctor's bill.

When the doctor passes his hands over the crystal ball later for the three of them, the husband of course is not inside. Instead they see two old stars appropriately costumed pressing their hands and bosoms against the glass, mouthing, I accept, I accept.

Two Dog High

He is shoveling the bags full. He is not one to run out and buy ten bags already filled so he fills them with the sand himself, one after the other. After all, you just empty them over the side, is how he sees it.

I sew them shut. With a needle this size. We never leave needles this size in the balloon's gondola, just in case. Hours and hours up there, with only prairie going under, you can be tempted by things, you may want to climb out or touch branches or even telephone wires—and a needle is one of those things you might want to touch. Touching wind is the most of what you should do in all those hours, to keep track of it, touching wind like the back of a lathered horse.

Herman shows up with his rig. It is still so dark I sew a sack to one of his sacks while his dogs set to. Named for their fighting style, they are called What? and Why Not? That is, one dog barks and the other answers. They always go up together, despite this obvious anger between them, despite the rules. They sort it out, says Herman who races solo to make up for their weight.

Why not take birds instead? They're lighter company at least, I say.

They talk, he answers over the dogs' back-and-forth barking. He tosses in bone treats, the thuds luring the quarreling dogs over to the balloon. Lifted inside, they bark even more but once aloft, they go quiet, stick their noses over.

Herman hangs above us, while we finish with the bags, and I go on about what I've read vis-à-vis the French and ballooning. They screwed all the time while they were up, I say, that's why they never set a record.

I don't believe it, he says. But that's an idea.

We have our own history and it is some history. The two dogs are nothing, barking and barking. He tosses his shovel into the back of the pickup and there is just light enough to see his face, the smile he puts on it for exercise.

Or maybe he likes the idea.

Anyway, the French used to love ballooning, I say. French women, especially.

Oo-la-la, he says as he lights the flame. Then whoosh, god-in-a-ball-of-light beautiful, that blueness, and we're up. The race proceeds elegantly, all of us and the rest from elsewhere, bobbing up and down in water, or that's how it always looks to anyone below. We soon fall way behind. Too much weight, I say, emptying a half bag over.

A loose inch sands our feet. Not so well sewn, he says but before I can compose my dark look, he says, Hey, it's the beach, get barefoot, and he empties the rest to our ankles.

We take control of a nice set of gusts and pass Herman by the time I remember the French again, one particular woman. A balloon caught fire, I say, and they were going down anyway, and it was just a question of how fast the descent as to whether they would be saved. That's why the Frenchman jumped out.

She asked him to, I'll bet.

He volunteered. The French invented chivalry.

She shoved him, he says and goes back to the gas dials.

He really loved her, I say over the loud jets.

Herman waves at us. The dogs are jumping and snapping, which always slows him down. It is his own fault this time—he holds a bit of meat in the air.

You should talk to Herman, he says.

Herman likes dogs, not girls. I turn down the cock.

He once had three dogs.

Go on, I say.

And he once had a girl. But she wouldn't come up.

He never said.

He saw somebody else's car in her driveway from up here. You know, you're not allowed to fly if you throw down something you shouldn't but I can see why he had to do something. Why, I think he's still looking for her—or that car—with the dogs he has left.

I watch Herman laugh at his dogs. Was it her dog? I say.

I don't know. It was just something I saw, he says.

You saw him do it?

He had two dogs when he landed. He told me about the car.

History is a cloud you don't see unless you look up and only now and then does it rain and make a difference. We have clouds. We even have rain at a slant in the distance. Okay, I say, but we're not like that.

Are you sure? he says.

We go way up and drift inside a cloud that doesn't stop, the gondola swaying and the fire above and as much noise between us as we want. We end up in Iowa or what seems like Iowa, a very long way from the chase cars.

After we tie up, we call Herman on the cell phone. He says everything is just fine and yourself?

I can hear the dogs barking behind his voice, just the two of them.

The Last Night

I am holding myself in my glass, my chin doubling in bent reflection, my neck moles floating. We are always wadded up or naked or torn at the liquor cabinet mirror, I say.

Don't look, says my husband.

Meteors shower gently over the undulant mountains that take up the distance. No one says the shower is a sign, just how goddamn pretty, though someone does go on with a black hole story, black holes coming to get you and all your meteors too and it is without an end, the story, the way a scary story should be.

I finish my drink and my self-scrutiny and evade the scrutiny of others by struggling with the sleeping bags, each tight bolt needing to fit back into the car somehow and still allow door access. My drink and its dregs reach into me while I reach and stuff and restuff.

He puts down his glass, the man I'm married to, not the one who's still going on about the black holes, he puts his glass down and takes out a pen and paper. Don't forget, he says, write about the sky coming apart, about the light on this.

Light? I say, not taking the pen. Say what you mean.

My husband refills his drink and not mine.

Is the future a kind of black hole? my son asks. The question takes on such a slant, with his voice growing quiet near the end as if someone's grading him or at least cocking an adolescent cynical head. But there are no adolescents here but him, not even in theory—his brother's—and the wind comes up then, more blackness rides in on the end of his words but no real new information, and nobody says Yes. Maybe they feel the future against them the way I do.

The bags are finally tucked.

We will not return here, that is the way people travel now, once here and once there, especially with time advancing like a backlit body in middle age, thick and jerky.

The reasons for not returning are clear enough.

My older son asks one last thing: this lighthouse behind us that leans—its leaning's caused by the last earthquake, not like Pisa's, he points out to his brother who is standing nearby on one leg only, the way children do, lighthouse-like—say this lighthouse, he says, is sucked into the black hole. Would it still put out light?

His brother takes a step back, really a hop.

The black hole man can hardly be seen as the light from the meteors is all gone and his back under his telescope is almost headless in the dark that a lot of trees make in this vacation place so close to the sea, but his nod is seen, my son sees it.

I won't see it soon.

I have a question too, says the littler son, hopping over to his sleeping bag swelling from the window. Did pirates worry about black holes?

The man puts the cap on his telescope—the eyepiece, not the electronically amplified eye. My husband should be staring into it next but he's turned to the black depths of the mountain the sleeping bags make against the slippage of the stars that no longer fall, and he's sipping.

Ha-Ha-Ha, pirates, says the older son very loudly. The littler one starts to cry: You're just making fun of me.

The older one smiles, the way you do if you have what I had in my glass, but he's drinking Mountain Dew, the soft hard drink. I think that's what he's drinking. Dad? he asks.

Those pirates lived when no one knew about black holes, says my husband. Not knowing skips the fear. You can't be afraid without knowing.

He knows.

The man behind him who holds the telescope cap like an O from a cereal, something explainable, says, Pirates kept track of stars more than most.

He pours more into my husband's glass.

In his voice I hear that the man doesn't care that we are not coming back, not even if he were to put his lips right you-know-where on me, which he has already done, in the bright light of yesterday.

Such a dark.

I am unruly with leaving, I am driving already.

He doesn't care if we don't get back over the mountain for most of the night. There are children here for godsake is what I said yesterday when I let him put his lips there, and there are still children. We've got to get going, I say, the children will miss their sleep. Good night.

Good night, he repeats.

This man has a burr in his voice which no one misses, my littler son asking the first day if he knows how he sounds because that's what his speech therapist asks him, but this burr is caused by the geography of his birth he tells my son and here, next to these mountains in the dark, the voice does its own traveling, goes deep into my desire.

You look long enough into that telescope, says my husband, and the cup pressure breaks vessels and you get a black eye.

This is such an oblique explanation of the man's eye that the kids laugh and even he does. Nobody has said what they could about that eye, that dark ring caused by my husband, and now we are leaving, we are walking into the dark and can't see his face and its darkness.

The lighthouse behind us turns on, with a *Boo-wah* and a shrieking of birdlife, this last made as a heron dodges the dark telescope my husband did look into once he knew where to look yesterday. How was I to know that the boys, bored, had refused, that my husband wasn't staring the way you stare at a sky with inquiry, but elsewhere?

The laugh we all make about him looking into that telescope helps us fit into the car. Soon we begin the mountain ride home into stars, the ones that have not yet showered, and I hold back tears that will be shed elsewhere on some other pretext, but that are always ready in case I want to think about what happens with a small family and a man with a telescope who doesn't charge us for all the drinks it turns out, and He damn well shouldn't is all my husband says as he guides the car through the switchbacks with me holding the receipt an inch from my nipple well covered and blind but, after all, still mine.

We Are Learning How to Talk

We are learning how to talk. Half-circle, group, now lined up with No-you-before-me at break time. The chairs could and do talk, unfolded as they are for everyone who comes late, screeching, metal on metal, the way the stories are volunteered, no apologies, and then there's this break, and we leave those chairs, all of us old-to-middle-aged parents, broken and sad and surprised to be hungry except for a sibling who is young, strawberry-cheeked but still spent, the way the glop on the break food that's pink is, the way the torn-apart sweet rolls taste, milk slopped beside coffee drip, coffee weeping to the floor.

Rage is more like it, we gape while others talk through their stories and then we rage through ours, we all need sutures. We have two minutes to tell everything to each other. It turns out to be a lot of time, rattling, rattling with heartbreak, years are involved.

The man beside me, his white hair fleeing his head in some smart way, his folding chair protesting his return from the break, is heavy with feeling. I lean into my chair, it squeaks and he thrusts himself forward in his with *Hello*. His son is himself wrought wrong, he has said, his son he cut into sentences so precise in his two minutes that he must be a surgeon: where's the scalpel for this? Where's the entry? Every tool points to the self is what he says now. His wife crouches at his flank in a chair that agrees, she lies in the wind of his report, the weather of it brisk and affecting, the words nodding, hers too.

His two minutes were the longest.

Each of us tried to up the ante: a son in a house for a year chained, finger by finger, to a computer, a daughter who wants nothing except what leads to a noose, another with rehab in series for his son, and buddy-buddy bondsmen, a parent who drives punched-out car windows, who has offspring of offspring who use. No one has bad children, children left out of the fridge and turned bad. Our children rage like us at themselves, and forget and then hurt us so big we parents shrink to fit. Also no one is rich after all the shrinks, or even before, with truant officers and then bail, so there's no envy, no monetary advantage.

The white-haired man stopped his two minutes with comments about lack of medical services and his shock thereof. The hospitals aren't Obama's by any means, but.

Everyone nodded then. I nodded. His wife beside him started leaking flat tears. Now she tips forward on her folding chair, almost on her haunches to say—

No one can hear her but we listen.

Again.

What? Her husband turns to her.

I'm afraid, she says too loud back. I ran to the bathroom to collect myself the way you suggested, she says to us, she bows to the leader who has stepped back into the room, strawberried, coffee-ed, and only too well aware of our problems, his own two children exemplars. He is the one to whom the cries of the chairs are directed, and he's often silent.

The boy's too big, she says, looking at her husband, not the leader. The boy scares me.

The husband narrows his eyes.

You have to use your delay, says the leader.

He was kicking in the door, she says.

I see, being closer, the dark under the cantaloupe foundation that is spread across her skin below her eyes.

The man with the seriously suicidal daughter, desolation incarnate but with surprisingly chipper clothes, says, Visualize otherwise.

When she swallows and goes on without words, just shaking, the leader says, You have to see these children with bolts through their heads—

That's not real, that's not real, she answers. Not a monster.

The white-haired husband dares to lay his hand on her shoulder.

I want to touch him, the gesture is so touching, but she flings it off, saying the son tried to kill her that day and that was why she fled to the bathroom and what is she supposed to do about that? He—and she jerks an elbow at the husband—says it's nothing, not to worry, he'll—what?—grow out of it?

She doesn't say all of that, some of that we insert, knowing what every sob signifies, amplifies, except for the kill part. She says out loud what we all fear, that instinct to kill the parent that runs along like a rat under the skin of all children, that instinct with the stink inside it that parents fear big, that these anomalies of the mind—are they really?—make it easier to see, in fact, with our children's better muscles and short spans of reason and their dark thoughts tangled by internal globs of newly hatched hormones, it is even easier to see how hard it is for them to resist this.

She has fallen off her chair, she is sobbing that hard.

The husband sits there.

The leader clamps both hands to her shoulders, the leader rocks her quiet until the husband says restraining order and protective services, then she uprights herself with a spring that the leader isn't balanced for, he sprawls, she's on her feet and yelling at the husband, against all his white streaming probably doctor hair.

I turn to my husband who doesn't hear the chairs or the coffee dripping at break or the leader when he does talk, although he does admire the leader for his job that he doesn't volunteer for. My husband is here in placation. It only rhymes with vacation. My husband said not a word about our son during our two minutes, other than positive. I admire this stance but words here and in this situation are for truth and not magic. This is the gist of the woman's lashing back, the black and blue marks on her arms she shows by peeling her shirtsleeves all the way to her armpits. Whatever she says about her son I remember nothing, I'm watching my husband's hands clench and ball.

She's a woman not wifed, not mothered, but troubled. Troubled is not the word. She has fallen to her knees and the husband is saying No the way a person, faced with a bad piece of themselves they grew on their back where even they couldn't see it, might on discovery. Not you-are-crazy-and-a-liar but a No-I-don't-want-to-know.

In fifteen minutes we spew from the room onto the dream of an institutional lawn: Adirondack chairs positioned in front of geese. Only the trees are weeping.

See? I say, shaking, and he says, at last, Yes.

The Long Swim

In Jamaica, all afternoon the dog dragged itself across the beach on his front paws, all the engine he had. That ocean had so much salt when he hit the water it kept his head up and he could swim in it.

Nobody believes me. Dog joy on my brain, I pull down my suit-crotch and slither into the pool we've rented with this condo in Florida. My chin up, my limbs flailing, I spot a pretty seashell on the opposite edge, its meat hanging out, an accusing red lump some kid left stinking in the sun. I dive, spreading pool water around, wondering how useful is a shell really until it is empty?

Not from the shell's POV.

Seven sets of toes line poolside when I've flung enough water off my eyes. Too many. Someone's supposed to be sleeping.

I never went for a swim in Jamaica, I couldn't leave the baby on the beach, I tell those toes thus lined up, but they tap and my brother says I am late.

His two sprites bob at an angle near where the sun is sinking so I can't see to grab one of their wrists to ignite a smile on him. They scream at someone else instead, being extracted from the pool against their out-of-proportion-to-their-size wills.

As to wills, my father sits lordly and dry in an overlooking room, conniving a quick trip to the gift shop to wed a woman in a short top—he wishes, he wishes, but commands us as audience for his will instead, says my brother.

But first, a photo. We line up against the foliage with shed water as shadows under us, the wet ones, we smile when told, when shot.

We are all wearing t-shirts with my father's brand across it, S with an arrow from its heart, to distinguish our herd. Until this photo of brand documentation is made, planes will be held for family members, no one will be allowed to eat, let alone swim. Pizza is what we say fast with our eyes closed against encroaching departure times, against pizza lust, against the aforementioned son.

I mean sun. I have nothing versus the son standing way at the back so he seems short, so tall he blots out the waning rays. Nothing, except for how he says everything is my fault. His birth is, but I'm not sorry enough about that to revoke the crazy joy of raising him, the sly six notes on the sax after I forbade him to practice. He kisses me goodbye, one peck before the airport taxi opens, and won't call and won't leave a number because how can you punish a mother any other way?

I drip. Will creatures crawl out of their shells at night if I don't appear at his side in the dark of wherever? It's a lot of heave-ho dragging if you have only one leg under your timber, the way I feel about him. Maybe flippers would speed the shell forward, I suggest to the two sprites with all their adolescent futures before them, who tease a crab. They shiver and dance on the cement with it, then vanish as quick as the crab.

My father is laying out his tricks when I arrive on his balcony, with cards, some of them—a few queens—so female you imagine them banned, out of play. I've changed my mind, he says. I am not giving you any of the money Mom left, but buying another farm like I've always wanted. Let's vote on that, he says. And approve it.

Everyone approves it but me and my vote is just token, I'm just one will against too many.

Now I want everyone to play charades, he says, collapsing his deck as if found fondling it.

My sister, only fifty-eight years old, leaps to the floor and bites her son's ankle. No props, screams my brother but we all guess— it's her vicious old dog. Then she flings herself into our father's lap and, while he lights up with anything female so close, we guess it's Tom, his doggie replacement for Mom.

Hey, this isn't charades, says someone who isn't close family or not close enough.

We just bark.

The two sprites can't stop barking and lie on their backs, pawing the air. Then there is ice cream or dream cheese on a bagel, then there is dessert on a stick. Wrappers find mothers who stick them under cupboards, inside bags, between drawers.

Who finds the flashlight, and another, and another?

Past all the screened-in rooms and foyers and verandas, we walk in single file—not pedi-, says someone in the dark—we walk toward the beach in this flat world of drive, we are walking to the sand that takes up where the boardwalk doesn't and the rotting sea life gets started. We spin our flashlights everywhere, having heard that turtles crawl onto the beach in the middle of the night, as anxious as we are to leave progeny behind.

Who said that? I ask over the loud laughter of someone play-golfing at the egg-balls the turtles are said to deposit.

Their hearts keep on beating after they're dead, answers someone else.

Such optimists, I say and put my flashlight in my mouth. It lights me, my mouth so wide and red I'm scary, I could be a beating heart. Love, love, love.

We stand ankle-deep in the sand, happier, not wiser, declaring the great amphibians clever to go on sexing it up under the water, keeping their eggs stuck in their slots and skipping their scheduled appearance on this beach. We ourselves have all reproduced, in cold or hot water or near it, and turn off our flashlights to have our hands free to toast each other in celebration, the thin plastic shells around the drinks making so little sound we go quiet and gulp.

It's instinct, says someone who isn't dreaming. See?

Beyond our sandy ankles a super-sized creature drags itself out of the rushing dark water, into the dark.

Decorum Stinks

I cut through their garden and break into their garage. Not true—
they left the garage door open. Night viewing, they called it, the
business door locked. Feel free, they told us, so I climb over their
power mower and feel free.

May already sits in a chair in the next room beside Mom.

He's right, the color isn't right, I say.

I've done my deed, she says, noodling Mom's lipstick in and out.
I brought the right one. I'm not putting it on.

The plaid suit we picked out suggests feistiness. For the archae-
ologists, I said earlier. We couldn't mention her troublemaking in
the obituary. The old lipstick now rubbed across her lips fights the
suit's color.

The undertaker pops in, dressed all track-suit-and-sneakers. What
have you brought me?

May hands off the tube, and another. Mom liked her mascara too.

His hands go up. I don't do lashes.

Isn't it included? I ask. From our POV, too little is, having been
dragged down here with new lipstick.

The question unanswered allows time for him to find and flex the
mascara's brushy blackness. How hard can it be? he says.

The light's kind of dim, says May, without optimism.

He twists up the fluorescence. We go from crypt to supermarket
bright to see him rubbing his hands together as best he can with
lipstick and mascara in one of them, mumbling something about
decorum.

Decorum stinks, says May. She says it twice, soft-then-loud, into the glare.

The undertaker blinks and bends to work on Mom's lips.

Not two minutes later, his mother shuffles in, wearing rubber boots.

She says our mother was an excellent bridge player. To make sure I understand how excellent, she nods her hair-sprayed head, a gesture of the deaf. Probably she'd gone deaf from decades of hairspraying.

Thank you, I say as if having played Mom's bridge games myself.

May stares at the old woman's rubber boots. I try not to. They are wet, you can see them glisten as she makes her way into the viewing area.

This color? she says of the lipstick, as if Mom's taste is in question, as if ours is questionable, as if we know nothing about what one wore on one's lips in such a social situation.

Tissuing the edge of Mom's mouth, her son ignores his mother. We worked on live models in Vegas last year, he says.

Botoxed? I ask.

He says, Yes, the skin is about the same, and his mother smiles, so pleased we know so much about their practice, then he quits with the lipstick and steers her back into the dark room she came out of.

In the interim we peek into where the rest of the chairs are arranged for the priest tomorrow. He'd begged: No eulogies please, people get carried away.

Of course they get carried away, May'd said, and the priest at least laughed.

When the undertaker reappears, May says, as if for instruction, Mom was given to pouting.

For a moment I mishear *shouting*, and look hard into a dark window, then back at our true subject, with reluctance.

Usually moving, Mom's lips-at-a-rest look creepy so smeared, as if caught in slo-mo. What he needs is a brush to fix them but he says they didn't use those in Vegas. He pushes the new lipstick across Mom's lips again and ruins them thoroughly, the color two-tone and lumpy.

At least nothing smells in here, says May, by way of encouragement.

He caps the tube and starts right in on the mascara, using it as if he's never seen a commercial or his mother wielding a wand of it, and leaves a track of black across her cheek. The utterance that follows approaches the vulgar and he briefly, ever so briefly, touches his head against the rock of Mom's forehead, in despair.

I pull a tissue from his box and hold it toward him.

While he rubs at Mom's face—will her skin rip?—his mother wanders in again and washes her hands behind us, as if of him. When she walks over this time, I get a glimpse of the something stuck to her rubber boot, and May stands.

Mission accomplished, says May, like Bush on a battlefield.

Goodbye, lipstick, I say, goodbye, Mom.

The undertaker and his mother flash us the smiles of people who always have the last touch, if not word.

The public exits from the viewing room are double. May takes the far door and I leave by the other. We head out so fast from our opposites we run into each other.

Knock yourself out, says May.

What would Freud say? I say.

We laugh until we cry, we do drive away.

Man Is Born to Trouble as the Sparks Fly Upward

Three motorcyclists rip through the gravel that Granny spread not the week before, spraying stones in a half moon along the house side. One of the bikers is not hers, the farm girl from Ohio. Ohio, the other two call her, a type of cigarette-smoking farm girl you didn't have too many of then.

Granny flicks her apron-tail catlike at their noisy arrival. She stands inside the screen porch while they stand their bikes like horses, sleeking their silvery haunches with the backs of their shirt-sleeves. At least Kermin does, the one so fastidious about cleaning chickens and who spends overmuch time in the washhouse. His brother hangs around Ohio to make sure her straps are solid around her saddlebag where she keeps dainties like wrenches, judging from the bulges. Granny hears him say, Granny is an old rosary fart.

The sun keeps the screen dark so unless she moves, she can see and hear more.

She won't want to go in on it?

I'll make sure, says Kermin, and he produces a smile that even in the hanging dust any woman could appreciate, a smile that signals to Granny he's put down some drink.

Granny light-steps the three steps into the kitchen backwards so as not to disturb her shadow. She has pots going and a general mess of living that preys upon her, she takes what old rosary she has inside.

Instead of making sure about whatever it is she might want to go in on, Kermin crawls under the house. Even at the sink, she can hear him at the used-up bottles. The other two are hesitating at the door, probably hot for each other, then they let it slam on the spring, Ohio calling out *Granny!* at the threshold as if she belongs there.

Granny lets her pat her hand so friendly. You have lungs after all that riding.

We shortcutted all the way from the backdoor of the movie house, across those fields that haven't been plowed, says the boy.

Errol Flynn does it that way, says Ohio.

You find out all sorts of baloney at a double feature, says Granny, going for a spoon hung on a nail across the room. What else would they say before they said what they wanted?

It is 1924, begins the girl. She nods to Granny as if she will contradict her. And March 12 in only three weeks.

That will make her twenty, says Kermin, coming in with all Granny's old bottles jangling in a box. The girl gets a party. He smacks the box down next to the sink.

His brother takes a long swig at the faucet and slicks back his hair with the water before it quits. We are only wanting a real nice party, he says to Granny.

Not my dandelion wine! says Granny.

She's a criminal, your own granny, says the girl, lighting a cigarette. A winemaker. That's what all these old bottles are for—evidence.

When they're full, it's really for the goats, says Kermin. The goats get sick and only two tea cups' worth of dandelion wine will cure them. He rattles the empty bottles like Granny's not listening hard enough.

I am always glad to see you, says Granny, not smiling. What about gravy on bread? I've got beans.

The girl smokes. The boys mouth something back and forth to each other as if they aren't going to say anything at all. We wouldn't visit much, is what Kermin says out loud at last.

That is a good thing, the way they put it. Granny holds little patience for their schemes, she says: What do you really want?

The brother unsnakes rubber tubing from his back pocket.

When you were a boy, says Granny, you stole one of those from the washhouse and flooded the place fooling with it. She turns her spoon bowl up and taps her palm. I guess I forgot to burn it.

So what I'm saying is, says Kermin after the girl gives him a *What now?* look, is that we want to set up a still for the party and make something for ourselves to boot. There is where we want to do it. He points to the bathroom.

I spoiled you, buying those motor bicycles with the wheat money, says Granny. She states this like truth be known. I should have paid my taxes instead.

The brother who is two years younger but bigger takes a step closer to Granny as if to persuade her with his size but she quick hits him in his eye with the spoon.

The boy screams.

Ohio and Kermin don't help him get over it, they back away, Kermin saying, For pity's sake.

The boy feels his way into the bathroom, bumping into the hamper on his way, cursing and blubbering. The girl picks up the hose he drops and lays it beside the kitchen sink, then she and Kermin start washing up the bottles beside it.

You won't need those for quite a bit, says Granny. Why not wash the bathtub?

Ohio laughs. She's probably got a recipe in there too, she says.

While they are in the bathroom setting up the still, arguing about where to put the worm box and who's getting the hog feed, and which of them knows best how to hook up the heat, Granny swings at the bottles with the hammer she keeps under the sink. The bottles are thick and old, she was saving them forever so it takes a good lot of whacking, two or three hits, before she gets to where some of them really fall apart.

Kermin wrenches the hammer away from her, but he has had too much to drink and the wrenching makes him fall backwards and hit his hand on the table.

You cut yourself, Granny says.

He sucks his knuckles and glowers. You keep out of it.

Granny laughs too loud.

His brother picks the few good bottles out of the bad and brings them along into the bathroom while they go about finishing their business. When they leave, they pocket its key. You've got Mr. Jim, they say, pointing to the outhouse.

The bottle shards lie in their patterns on the floor for weeks after, which disturbs Kermin more than his brother when they next visit, bursting into the kitchen the way they like to. Darn stubborn old hen wants us to clean up, he tells Ohio, coming in last. She is wearing a short skirt this time, all the way up to her knees, which, when dismounting the motorcycle, is its own show. Now they have only the two bikes, Kermin having broken a spark plug roaring over the rutted fields. He needs to collect some profit for its repair, birthday or no birthday.

While he looks around for a broom to sweep away the shards, his brother picks his way through them. Granny? They haven't been around to check up on her. She doesn't answer back. He unlocks the bathroom anyway.

Don't do too much stirring, says Kermin, drawn past the broom closet to the bathroom.

You don't want scum, says Ohio, and she goes ahead and stirs and then swallows several sips that send her throat into spasms.

Sure you're not born this very day? asks the brother, who is trying to fill the bottles while taking two sips to her one.

Soon Ohio is touching the silverware, the little knickknacks, the towel for drying, and the brother's elbow. What if she's dead? she says, without a trace of concern.

Kermin has his share even quicker and is now beating his chest like the ape in the movie last week, and howling. That should wake the dead.

But Granny doesn't come running.

I'm hungry, says his brother, stepping around the unswept shards to Granny's ice box. Nothing in here, he says, drawing two fingers through the soft butter. Just this, and some old milk. He flicks the latch to the food safe beside it, a screened-in cupboard for cake and sundries, and pulls out a piece of actual cake, or something cake-like in weight and shape. He gnaws half of it down before Kermin can scrounge up a knife.

The girl overturns her glass on her chin and tries to balance it there, her eyes crossing. Kermin touches the glass with the knife, and it falls. You might go blind doing a thing like that, he laughs, and stirs its shards in with the others.

Then I wouldn't have to see you, she flirts back.

A neighbor who has given Granny a lift backs out of the driveway fast, seeing the motorcycles. Granny isn't carrying much, just some papers she's signed at the courthouse, but it isn't the lack of a burden that keeps her from galloping up the steps as if she were excited to see them. She puts down her purse in the weeds and waits.

Even the crickets go quiet.

She could walk the two miles back to her neighbor's but it is very hot. She waits longer. She reads over the signed papers to make sure who gets what, and who doesn't.

Kermin comes out and vomits beside the front door. Hello, Granny, he says, getting up off his haunches.

I am sorry I raised you, she says. I wasn't fit for it. I spoiled you because I was too old or else you were rotten to start with.

Kermin smooths a curl of saliva into his pant crease. By the look of his face, he is still distressed about his stomach. Did you put rat poison in the cake?

I did, says Granny. There were rats, there was a hole in the safe.

We don't want to call the sheriff about it, says Kermin, and he lets her in.

His brother is laid out on the glass shards. Granny starts talking, talking, talking about what to do. The pigs ate the fermented apples only once, she says. They never touched them again. Why can't you boys be more like pigs?

Shut up, says Ohio, who did not have any of the cake, who instead has drunk a whole glass of hooch on her empty stomach for full effect, who is loose in the legs now, and skittish and unconcerned.

Granny says: Pepto-Bismol's under the bathroom sink.

Kermin unlocks the bathroom a second time. Or else salt, shouts Granny. Lots in a glass. Put it down him. Or else the milk.

No milk. Kermin drank it all with his piece of the cake, neatened where his brother left teeth marks. He is swallowing a glassful of saltwater himself in the only container Granny hadn't filthied, a gravy boat, so she gets ahold of one of their almost full bottles and empties it into the sink for another. Kermin chokes and bellows and Ohio lunges at her, but misses. She pours the salt into the bottle with water, and puts it to the boy's cold lips where it dribbles out and then in, when he coughs and spits.

Kermin is gargling more saltwater by then, the girl patting his ankle, the girl being on the floor and about to pass out.

Granny clears the boy's mouth and douses him again. Did you like the cake? she shouts.

She's a monster, says Ohio who rallies and staggers to the door for her motorcycle. Happy birthday to me, she says outside on the porch, then past it, about to straddle the seat, her skirt to her waist.

The boy is unconscious again before Kermin takes off, with the girl driving. But they only get as far as the cherry tree before a low branch knocks them both clean off. Granny doesn't bother to turn them over, seeing the flutter of somebody's limbs. They will be all right. The toppled motorcycle chugs until the gas runs out. She is still standing on the porch when the ambulance and the sheriff arrives, spraying their own gravel.

Haven't seen you in a long while, says the sheriff, prodding at the boy in the kitchen while the ambulance people set up. What's all this glass from?

Another accident, she tells him quick. I got a little upset with the boys.

He nods as if he expects it so. She puts on her apron and starts a slow sweep. I'll have it up in a minute, she says. She doesn't want anyone here long enough to want the bathroom.

The Haight

It isn't as if we are close, only her sweater is. It still has her shape from so much of her in it before I took it. I left first, and I knew what cold could await me. That she might leave too was not my problem. She had a place with my mother, she painted my mother's nails, she stood behind her couch and pressed her fingers into her forehead for headaches. I made up so little of that life, I figured they wouldn't miss me, I figured her sweater as a souvenir of what I wouldn't miss.

Her underwear too. A baseball cap. I took enough of her things so I didn't look her up a year later when I barefooted it through her town, or at least the town where Mom said a boy with airbrushed tattoos and teeth you could count had taken her. I had had enough of those boys myself, let alone the sweater I had worn and worn without looking her up and saying I'm sorry. It's the least you could do, said my mother, but I did less.

After another year passed and hunger wasn't as new as all the other new things, I happened again to visit her town and Mom said, Check, just check up on her, I haven't heard boo from her for six months, but I didn't. I said I work now, I conference all day, and at night I sleep hard. Which wasn't all true, I was stuffing computer specs into the trash instead of smiling cow-eyed at brochure-laden retailers wearing actual patent leather, then getting wasted at nights at concerts and at last, laid, by nobody business.

I was tired.

The next time I flew there I was up to my neck in green screens, a look-see so new most of them were cardboard. Mom didn't care to hear about my trials ordering these screens for all of my twenty-four clients. She said when she herself had flown there, the address was all wrong, it could not be right, and she found out nothing.

She must have moved, I said. She knows where you live, I said.

You're the only one to find her, you look like her, she said.

I would recognize myself if I saw me? I said.

She went quiet.

I don't have that sweater with me, I laughed my best fake laugh. I need the sweater as a lure.

That Mom should still be bothering, after all my sister's silence and not mine, hurt me. Who says one sister and another makes two together?

When you consider I was searching for a livelihood and someone to keep it lively all those years after, I was busy. Mom kept busy knitting more stinking sweaters—not for me—and for Mom time was just a stitch dropped, or another color of yarn. Then music we heard before came back, like we were always tuned in but turned down, but my sister didn't. No letters with postmarks stained from rain or backed-up sinks left any kind of trail, no phone calls rang, charges reversed, there were no phone calls at all, the silence continued like a skip at the end of an old 78, a silence even I had to notice.

Did anyone know where the tattoo king had come from, exactly where he might leave for? I asked. He ordered pizza to go and your sister went with it, said my mother. She ordered the pizza like it would bring her back, got old with that pizza and didn't eat it, made phone calls and aggravation and sweaters, and then died without a word from my sister.

I cut my hair short the way she wouldn't, I kept away from pools and mirrors of all kinds so I didn't think *Who else?* when I looked. But now crowds crowd around in the new malls with glimpses of my sister everywhere. I decide I must go, I must find her, I must ask her what she thinks she is doing.

The Haight is the place where someone like her with a pizza eater of tattoos and few teeth would end up at, that's what my mother always said about that town that all the buses led up to. Look at the map, and the cost of those buses, the kind of girl she surely turned into as soon as she left us.

So I go right to that spot and I put up and look at what pictures there are. The man at emergency pleads innocent, nada, no computers back then except for salary, and the police ask about tracks, did she have them? They didn't lead to us, is all that I answer.

The sweater I stole still fits me.

I'm looking for myself, I tell people. We have the same features. People smile and shake their heads. A lot of you came here, they say, the street was full of you, in and on it, people slept on people, humped here under the dark lights someone was always making here, the bulbs out all over. You couldn't walk the street like you do now, from one end to the corner.

What I find out, after all these years, is that anyone could be her—one of those with her head down, with no other reason than not to be seen, or with her head too far up, a big bird flying away with her brain.

A dog that is hers, or could be, can't find the hydrant he is so old. I take a place over the street and I watch that dog every day walk past my window. If she still comes to sprawl, one jeaned-leg crossed over the other the way girls her age did then, then this is where to watch. Otherwise, it's just a block not too far from a park.

I sit at the window in her sweater and she has my life now, bangs, a girl/boy/girl, wearing an apron no woman still young should wear, with Mexican shoes in green leather, and a husband who worked so hard he died early and left money. Or maybe she's not me—she could be the woman next door who moved out before I could ask about her tattoo and the pizza, or she could sell cars at a lot down the street during the hours I sleep.

Police and the places that follow her kind of problem still send me papers. See the papers? My mother had so many that the heat of their fire took the hair off my arms. They send me more papers whenever I ask about her so I'm sure there's someone with the same name doing something.

But not her.

Haight means hate, my sister getting even. It's just a sweater, I say. She didn't have it that long before I left.

To find me?

To be me.

Surprise! They say memory is all you are after you die.

She's done me one better.

Swanbit

Solely and thus sorely did he row the long distance off the disk of the sun into the dark of the piling-held dock where many-legged water creatures and not just water life lived, where he lived, being someone's extra son, when he could. For $54 a month he rented the boat, the tackle, the winsome boxed flies in inky camouflage, but what he really paid for was the dark under the dock and the water creatures with their habit of crawling or clinging to a lower region that confounded him, where mornings, he reached down and pried and sliced open and ate through the variously mollusked and non-mollusked on his own.

He was not mad. He could not get out of his boat without a winch, commercial or otherwise, being legless. The charitable called him cripple, but born without, it was not a case of crippled from, but just himself, crippled. He towed himself into the best spot under the dock and grasped at water life, its greeny shoots as misplaced or misaligned as he, and he became mad.

Starfish, crab, spider, but not the minnow, he decided in his madness—the limbless minnow was not fair game. He left the minnow alone. If, while hauling up one of his catches, he tipped the boat too far and overturned, he, in his madness, hoped for the fish to save him, to help him swim even better than he did with his strong arms like extra oars. A dolphin with a saddle on its back wasn't what he expected but some fish floating under his exhausted middle, nudging him ashore for all his pains taken, those many crab hooks unbent around all those gills. No way could he remount his boat himself if he overturned, he needed at least a leg over.

Birds that knew of his limblessness followed his rowing, or stood off, waiting, or dove at his bait and tried to steal it. He grabbed for them, declaring them armless, the wings faux as limbs. From the water, with such arms as he had from having no legs, he could grab the birds easily and had, catching quite a few ducks, and eaten them plucked and grilled over an iron pot lid filled with coals. This time—in this fogbound, dark afternoon—he grabbed and caught quite a big bird. Not that he had set out to. The bird had hissed and snapped at him and his six inches of crab bait, had hissed and snapped as if it were going to take the bait right out of the crab pot and sever his line, hissed and hissed until he hissed and snapped back. The bird lowered its neck at that, and so did he, while the boat floated closer.

A lot of neck on that bird, a neck that could span the reach, real swan. Mute? This bird spoke, wings breaking his grip, its beak leaking hiss.

The battle went thus: the man sprang at the bird, oar and arm. The bird caught the oar blade in its beak and held on, the man levered it almost out of the water then the bird, with a twist, tipped the man off his boat where he was perched, legless, in his absurd hissing pursuit of its fine stuffing and roasting.

The bird was bent double under his arm when he came up for air. Then its neck like a lamppost lost its height and its middle went under with his own weight centered over it. The man rode, he held tight, and enough that the life of the bird matched his own in danger that they swam together possessed, toward the boat that the tide was taking an interest in. The swan's wings broke his grip, its beak snapped: *let's swim*, its big feet flapping.

He was hungry.

The swan kicked with vicious complaint and the man grabbed it by the neck, then the bird curled around and bit the man so hard on the ear he bled. But still they kept hold of each other, the man to keep afloat, the bird in spasms over such a catch. When they met the current, both man and bird sank twice, and when they floated over the current-made shoal, the bird, sinking again, gashed at his arm until he let go, cursing and flailing, he let go and chose the shore to swim for. The bird chose elsewhere. Toward a fish perhaps.

It was a far shore. What fish saw him?

By the tide turn, the boat made land, the bait sticky-rotten and the second oar dragging in the lock. The worry and tick of fishermen who feared seeing him in themselves, belly down in a crawl from the pushchair still parked at a beach they infrequently frequented, propelled them to pull the boat in a week later, cutting at their lines with its shiftless float, its number soon enough pried off and scrubbed and painted blank all over.

Why didn't they look for him? A man with such loneliness repels even the moon's face in water. He could swim, they said. They had seen him.

The swan circles, some say, a certain spot.

Ottawa

A doorway is shadowed by a man I might know, or might have known in a memory that is washed by rain I make myself, a little cry, a misting over of time. I think I have a whole day to wander about this foreign city, all shadow and lag, so I skip the conference, I walk the sturdy bridges with fine landscape underneath them all wet and steamy, so pleased with the flashback machine under my umbrella putting out a fog that forces itself through the struts with their little huffs of dope-smell. I'm in Canada where anything retro can happen.

French pastry's in evidence down all the alleyways, regional chocolate cake revolves, roast lamb turns on spits—I turn too because I hear a dog bark—he had a dog—but in my turning, the bark fades as if I've imagined it. Did I? I'm trapped now, listening. Let another dog bark, or the same one.

Nothing. I walk another street beside the banks the fog hugs. Dinner with him would be perfect in an hour. I give him that long to turn up, the ache of being alone with food looming, with no other desire—liar. There are phone books to look into in the ensuing wait, there are the locals in his field who say no, they would have heard of him, and Google googles nothing. There's only history left, history other than ours—he could wash by as a corpse from another century, fall from a sailing ship stuck here for the winter by the creep of coming ice, have six children hitting him up for cash in a Canadian garret—or he could be sitting in a hotel room overlooking the atrium, awaiting me.

I mine a museum. I'm sure the mitten exhibit, as advertised on bright tricolored flyers, would lure him, or there's nothing like seeing whales cut open according to the sea museum's guide, or how about a diorama of grain elevators up the official escalator? I circle the pleasures of seeing: here is where I am now, here it happened once for us too, although nothing in the mishmash of the city's renovation leaves a scrap of where behind. No souvenirs. Exhausted, I settle on a place to eat, one that decorates with TVs, all tuned to bonfires. An ancient symbol of desire, a veritable chassis aflame—it's a kind of Hoary Welcome. Its distraction attempts to make up for the entree, dead-fish-on-a-platter, no parsley. I fork into it and pay and try another restaurant. But not after scrutinizing the revolving cake and meat menus of six others, peering through the windows at the crowd beyond. No doubt he eats at home. I settle on an appetizer of Brussels sprouts, a favorite of his. It comes doused in maple syrup of course, several sprouts cut into rose-shapes. I eat those first.

I could stay up all night, walk the streets, peer into what few nightclubs Canada's capital offers. I could sleep. That's closer to my desire, that's the same landscape—surrender, in the aged sense. I could tell the blank-faced concierge who waves at me on my return, I am meeting someone, and break my imagined allure with the only man so far who has greeted me here in this city of no surprise.

With maple syrup still on my breath, I brush my teeth, and discover the shower is without hot water. The concierge sounds so pleased to tell me I must move to another floor, it's as if at least he's been waiting for my call. He'll bring a key.

He takes his time. Damp and rapidly cold, I telephone downstairs again. On hold—love that term, so sensuous—I spot steam escaping outside, a veritable Scheherazade of steam, I know that hot water's out there somewhere, and him.

But it's the concierge who growls, *Venir!* through the slit in my door and leaves the key, clinking, outside. No apology. I remove my sticky soap from its alcove, and take the elevator with just the towel around me, nightgown in hand, scandalous, fully prepared to practice my excusez-moi in Canadian understatement. But non, everyone else is happy inside their hot-watered rooms, no one, not a soul, lingers near the elevator, hoping to catch such a glimpse.

When at last water surges hot and steamy into this new tub, I slip in the excitement and fall. I'm scalded, hair to toes, and skin my knee.

Now I am curious how much longer I have to dwell in this state of Canadian exile, this not-quite-right part of my remembered continent. Limping back to my room, I retrieve my small print program and it reveals the total error of my travel, mine and the organizer's, the slot for my speech changed, opening and closing while I was mooning around town, self out of self, for someone who existed solely in the window's reflections, and mine.

See the cross over the river of my morning's airplane so far above it—isn't the hairshirt of memory something we wash and then put on again?

Ha. With your mouth full of water, say Ottawa. That's how close I was to him.

Frangipani

Singular, the way each male member of the expedition keeps his face serious before pulling on the joint. Well, yes, it is their last, and blessed be whoever digs up a dealer here, so many thousands of miles across the ocean. The language alone.

But the locals speak the same one. The explorer with the roach is explaining the real root of their problem: we must think *island*. Weed has got to be hidden around here somewhere.

My lover agrees. He's tied a vine to his ankle and is going to throw himself over a cliff at dawn in twelve hours, along with three of the locals. They have to be stoned to go over the cliff, he says.

Or stupid, I say.

To a man, they turn to me, my guilelessness, my personal political dumb straight femaleness reveals itself once again and they make no comment, the worst.

The leader, who was the last to see Rockefeller before the crocs got him, suggests I go eat bread in case I still feel like vomiting.

I was going to say he ate the fish too, but okay. I get it, I'm leaving. Except that the painter of the expedition is sitting cross-legged in front of the door staring at his painter hand instead of moving aside. I make a motion to kick him. The guy beside him, the one with the vine around his ankle, my lover, shrugs with the *c'est la vie* he's all about.

I kick at the painter.

Through the window there's a color riot about to rot, the black and white world of night seeping into green birds, red blooms, swarthy brown pigs, sky broken up into islanders going about the late day business of drink and sex, and telling stories I can't get over: the ocean's orgasm so strong waves wash to the mountain top, the stars that fall down and roast a pig. I've only read translations. Otherwise, the locals are inscrutable, stamped, however, with kindness, and they dance and fish in boats badly now that we, in the royal sense, have landed our own and conquered and, in particular, have come to document their aforementioned.

I'm the sound girl of the expedition. The instrument I wield steals the souls from their drums, the usual. The rest of the expedition work the cameras and throw themselves—well, one of them—off cliffs to either show the locals that we are stupid too, or to demean their feat. The locals dance or fish when they feel like it and thus the cameras poke everywhere, and my baton of a mike too. Friendly enough, they don't eat us like they did in the good old past, but they could. These men I'm with—strange, I am the only woman, the locals have noted—these men gather every night after their cameras break down or run out of film or get too heavy, and they smoke and boast and plan the next day's shoot and whatever feat they feel they need to amp their big adventure, as if it is not enough to poke around all day in the local's.

Caught in all that slow-motion smoke, I think therefore I am— lonely. The lover with the tied-up ankle makes making love into exercise. It's a long way from home and the short relationship we had before we left. The others in the expedition are little curious about such an arrangement. I am best silent so when I do speak, they're astonished, the dog can dance, etc. I should be sitting next to the stoned lover and holding his what?

I kick the painter again.

Released at last from the smoky room, I practically dance. I would like to dance like or with the locals, with sex in every swerve, but I don't have the knees.

At the end of my walk into the dark, the ground goes hot, the litter of coconut and its leaves is much thinner and the locals ahead are flapping at me with warning gestures from flashlights. There's a pit that ends with a long trench, where a row of carcasses smoke—dogs. All the officials in the throng around the smoked dogs are very cheerful. The dogs always run into the road, says the prime minister-doubling-as-a-fireman, offering me a drink. Public safety, he tells me, is paramount.

The paramount chief in some place in Africa, I tell him, is smothered so he doesn't die a natural death.

He says they must smother these chiefs in bed, implying by his smile that is not a bad way to go. I smile back because what else? I accept a drink, a half coconut shell filled with milk and liquor. The roasting smells great, but I think of Fido, all the little Fidos, so foolishly domestic. The prime minister asks, Why isn't this being filmed?

I could say no one's going to rush out of their drug-induced stupor for a public safety ritual. The scene is barely lit anyway: the smoldering fire and torches of flame, the batteries of the flashlights on flicker. I am surprised when the painter shows up to beg for his own coconut cup of hooch.

Are you ready to go tomorrow? All packed? I ask him.

In some ways Gauguin never left, he says.

I roll my eyes, only inside my brain.

After the dive tomorrow, the expedition will fly away, all except myself and the lover. If the lover lives, of course. I refer to the lover as "the" to put some distance between my fear he might die and his fear I will leave him. You will kill me if you leave me, he says. He is going to beat me to it with this ankle thing. After the rest of the expedition leaves, we're supposed to shoot the intimate life of the locals together.

The painter says he senses my difficulties with the intimate life. In his experience, he says, an island magnifies them. The smaller the island—

He puts his arm around my shoulder. All my naïveté pushes into my mouth, not just the saliva of fear that someone has noticed the lover's manipulation of me, confirming that it is happening, and not fear that this painter is hitting on me for his own pleasure, since no locals have joined him in his hotel room, despite invitations, or so he says. Did you know, I say, these flowers—I shake off his arm in the act of pointing—are most fragrant at night, but they have no nectar and dupe their pollinators?

There are always two sides to a story, he laughs. I have a spare room in Phoenix, for instance.

I am nothing if not loyal, I am no one if I leave someone. I don't have bruises yet. What I answer the painter isn't the thanks for saying something.

I walk back.

All at once it is the next a.m. The men, minus one, point their lenses at the three locals and our one, all of them vine-tied. Will worry about the vine breaking go over the cliff with the lover? He doesn't care that I'm worried. He could care less. He is there, poised and stoned, with frangipani in a wreath around his head. Fragrant enough, he takes two steps and leaps over the cliff.

His ankle isn't even sprained.

Then the airplane flies off with the painter in it, an animal in the sky that is fleeing the cinders of the roasted dogs, more or less, my translation unfaithful.

What am I being so faithful to? Adventure. I am as bad as the rest. What did the lover do months later to trigger whatever letter I sent to the painter that he sent me a telegram, again offering exit? Did I write *Help* on a piece of paper and put it in a bottle? What I remember is the rain of the island forcing the rats into the bedroom.

Now I want to tell the very end of the story, about how I learned the lover was finally dead so many decades later, finding out three years after the cancer took him, about how he refused treatment, how he had no money anyway, no insurance. All those years he paid no taxes or rent, had no social security card, no email, no gas bill. The widow he never married had his five sons put his body into the back seat of a borrowed car and then they drove into the night to another state where they dug a hole. He told her he would wake her from her sleep for the rest of her life if she didn't follow his orders. Haunt, he said, the way he said it to me.

The Movie Business

The Torpor Inn. Surely. She opens a drawer to see how worn the Bible is, to see its gold edges half gone. Instead, a cockroach waves lazily from inside the un-airconditioned raw pine drawer, a jet-lagged gesture.

She doesn't need that drawer, she's just here for a day. She lays her dress over the room's hot chair and when she removes her shoes, she sets them on its seat as if cockroaches can't reach.

Nude at Noon. Great title.

The bedclothes fit.

Two men outside her window, in whispers she doesn't always get, she skips, she hears dubbed in her dream: All you do is get another bank account. You move it along.

Two men in a truck full of money moving toward her in the nude, with her casual in her corner room, sleeping, not sleeping.

Six thousand pounds of it, he says, and the money's in La Cienega's Citibank. All you have to do is pick it up. Nobody will know.

The men pour money on her.

· The bank number is—

What, she can't hear, or she does but she doesn't have a pencil, a pen is in her purse so far across the room. Don't they know she is asleep?

Heat holds her eyes shut, then forces them open. She kicks off the covers, she showers in the buggy bathroom under water that switches to cold and back while she stays soapy.

If she hurries, she will sweat, and sweat isn't cool. She sits beside the louvered window where the men had talked, minutes, hours? earlier opposite. If she'd only written down the bank number.

She needs money for her film.

If only her film needed just a box of electronics and a computer, but there are actors involved. She admires other people's economy, their clever single sets, their animations, their monologues, but she will conquer actors.

Expensive actors who don't act in the nude.

She pulls on her clothes, pulls and drags them over her sweaty legs and arms. Gray clothes, nothing stagy, but not too Californian, as if she mocks them, their bright desert light and bland color choices. Another cockroach feels along the beige wall toward the off-white louvers.

Half the film deal has happened already but the bank has balked. The money needs maturing—as they so parentally put it—for another two weeks. She needs more now. The sets, the unions, the costumes in alteration, the actor with his mother to minister. And herself.

She empties her shoe of its roach. She will take a bigger cut this time, even if it isn't on paper, even if it takes from props. There are appearances to keep up—she directs a little movie of herself, with cell phone locales, she makes ice clinking sounds with her comb and turns the tube to the porn station with its classical music before she dials and says, We're on for two?

Yes. Still.

She stuffs her purse: Tampax, two lipsticks, one hardlipped, the other more matching. She tosses out the Kleenex she used on the spark plugs. The borrowed Mercedes has TB, it coughs and bleeds. She will use the Tampax on it, in time. Keys, notes, comb, plane tickets.

She'd never live in this town. Her flights are strictly kamikaze, grab the cash and run or burst into flame. She knows people sense this, envy her for not having to live in situ. But they too grab.

Her lover calls as she backs out around two backpackers—the drug dealers with the bank number? Her lover tells her twelve details about his a.m. trials, all fortunate.

Palms begin to pop into place.

She will be too late if she drives down La Cienega. She is putting the whispered bank numbers into scene 5 when she reaches the address and they take her car. Valets, repo men, whatever—they come at her car too fast when she pulls in, as if she shouldn't be driving.

If their tip is too much, the amount makes her feel less fragile, more moneyed. Never ask for money without any to give away. Five moneymen are meeting her, she knows two. One from a fling from too long ago in the same office, now flung into the arms of a woman once a friend, another she knows from a banker who has only shaken hands with her in a lobby and nodded. She made much of that banker-meeting to his friend but it isn't epistemology, this kind of knowing. The rest have their reasons for being, all terribly benign, terribly power-ridden.

The film is beside itself, that is, only strategy will save it, not scenes on a drive. Earrings in place, cleavage enough to make them think twice, sex and money.

Cleavage: the cave woman's club.

But it is their club she enters. Minions hidden behind the pastel walls of the office speak softly, ever so softly, into their headpieces of her coming. She feels back in the movie 40s with secretaries plugging in calls, she smiles and rehearses an opening:

I will be clear.

She opens and opens, waiting. Green light it or cut it loose is another. No more limbo, no more lunch. She will be strong.

The headpieced woman—call me Sara—leads her at last past the office art into where they are meeting, outdoors on three sides, such bright light she shakes hands with silhouettes.

To have her hands free, she puts her purse on the table. After the nodding and the small talking standing up, as she bends to sit, one of the men already pulling out her chair—her friend, the banker's acquaintance, not her ex-lover, who isn't there—the other man on her left overturns her purse.

No, he picks up her purse and empties it across the table.

The lipsticks roll. The Kleenex and notes and pencils, the Tampax, the keys, the cell phone.

There, he says. Now we know who you are. He puts his hand into the pile and touches it all.

The others laugh, men with short haircuts and sleeves, men with nothing bald yet, men with gold rings.

With one arm she scoops at it, lets some of it fall off the table.

Gentlemen, she says.

Light crosses the room, a flashy car parking. One of the men—the banker's friend—picks up the Tampax and places it on the table.

The airport feels chilly but she would never pack a sweater for this trip, in this season. She stands in remote parking, shivering, she stands with her bag at her feet. Money moves somewhere—in her direction? She won't know for a while, though she has whispered the account number into one of the headpieces in case they don't have it. They will let her know. They know her.

Christ and Three Geese
and What Happened to the
Boy Afterward

They are not twins but sisters, though they like to match when they dress, when they do dress, that is, when a robe will not do for the little door-answering life they live, the door left open and the salesman or postal deliverer blinking at whatever peignoir meets him, a floating pink something. When they shimmy out of these, they wear dress suits and sensible shoes, so sensible that a clerk once said they could cross the continent in them, if the laces didn't give.

Then he sold them hide laces.

In the old home movies they love to watch, the elder sister dances in her own shoes, neither the sensible nor the peignoir but what you wear with a tutu. She dances all the right steps, showing them off to the father not shown, who works the camera. Later she wears the tutu shoes to beauty contests and maybe she wins them and more often she doesn't, according to her sister. This sister keeps the sensible shoes because two pairs are bought for less. However, she has been known to refuse to walk altogether or else will walk right on through the door in said peignoir and belt the mailman in the chops for being so forward, for taking the postage due, in her opinion, too slowly.

Their mother—the single one they have, and who needs more?—stays in her room and does not insist on warmed crackers or seeing the milk poured from the carton, not the way the girls say she does. That odd bit of a life in which the girls appeared—a brother too—has more to do with the grandmother who rosaried the mother into a gasp of marriage than with the professor-husband who quickly shook them off and died of drink. Now amongst the TV dinner droppings and the pitchers of water—this is an earthquake state—the mother keeps her ups and downs to herself, as much of herself as her daughters will allow, as much as they can complain and still roll her around in her mechanical chair, mechanical they call it, not wheel.

The boy had waited in the boy's room, dressed but never answering the door. He kept a dog who peed when petted but still required walks which he took, the boy dragging the dog begging to be petted out into the baked block of whatever sunbelt they had moved into. This relieved the dog, yes, but the boy more.

In their youth, no other children inhabited those just-asphalted perimeters of the cities they relocated into with what little money the professor had left them. Other children make noise and trouble, said the mother. A girl will attract traffic and a boy might throw a ball through a window and which would you want? The boy didn't have any balls to throw but did know boys who did, bad boys but not by name, anyway not by their given names but by the ones his sisters used, pointing them out at a distance, boys who lived somewhere in the cities they lived alongside.

The dog was a big white fluffy affair, about as peignoir a dog of that size could be, the only kind his sisters would allow, although the boy only saw its black tongue and the way it closed its eyes just before being petted. Men could not so easily get past the dog after the door-answering because of its size, men could not then take advantage of women not quite ready for proper presentation, though the younger sister fell into prayer for extra measure: Oh, my god, don't let him have a letter I have to sign for.

Men are not the point of the elder sister's beauty contests. Her talent in those contests for beauty has always been money and dance, not seduction, unless dancing for her father counts in that category. She dances for money with partners with blue boleros and very tight black satin pants who turn up their pinkies when they twirl her. She needs the money, but the little she makes after the cost of the costumes does not add enough to the little money the father has left, though she dances hard. They have all okayed law school for the boy to earn more. The father had taught at that school and when the son is admitted, he grows a beard like his father's at the end of his face, a scraggle of face hair that grows as if it is left over from somewhere else, someplace better for hair.

The girls shave it off him one night, the elder bearing down, with the younger holding his arms behind him with arms she has built up, the way they do on TV, lifting cans of beans instead of weights high over her head. The brother weeps through the shaving but their mother, rolling herself in, laughs at him for weeping, tells him to be a man. Or whatever.

He hasn't been in practice for more than twenty years before he marries his secretary. She's after his money, whispers the elder sister to the assembled, pushing the mother up the aisle in a corsage and purple veils, all smiles. She's got him by the bullocks, says the younger, a little louder. He'll take up drink like his father, they tell the justice of the peace.

Lips are sealed.

Since the two girls hadn't managed to get out of their robes to get to the rehearsal the night before, none of the bride's party has had the pleasure of inspecting the groom's. They stun: the elder still sports quite a bosom and legs, and has selected a low cut short sheath bearing polka dots of the clown kind, dots meant for viewing from stadium seats at a contest. Her face she's covered with pancake makeup until all the expression underneath slips around at the lipstick and lashes. A large rhinestone butterfly lights up her false blonde chignon, in accent.

The younger girl glitters, she French-twist glitters, shoulder glitters, eyelid glitters, she glitters with whatever catches in the net of her strapless, full-length ball gown. The late afternoon light, golden in this season of suburban fruition and waiting, reflects every millimeter of every square of the glitter. Her taut, bean-heaving biceps glitter.

An usher leads them to the front, to the groom's side. Stragglers from the bride's side fill out theirs. The two sisters twist around to see who is watching but everyone is discreetly looking elsewhere. The two of them use compacts with mirrors to find the bride's eyes as she walks up the aisle, to blind her with light. But their brother is getting away anyway, there is no doubt about it. The two girls comment on the flowers, the choice of ring, the sermon, the length of his pants, and then it is over.

But it is not over for the elder sister. First the bride's father croons a little song he made up the last time he saw her, a diaper-changing song, if not prenatal, and then the bride and groom dance and then her parents dance, his mother sitting in her chair smiling, although not idiotically—she knows enough to roll herself into the ladies right after. Then the music speeds up and those with drinks set them down and dance, surrounding the bride and groom who move as if they are alone, theatrically alone, slow against the fast beat, and the elder says: I know the man's part, and she puts out her hand for her sister.

Her sister takes it.

All glitter and dots, the two women clear the floor with their precise wide turnings and leanings-back, both faces grim or professionally pleasant. Where is the father to watch? Where is his camera? When the dance ends, as much as they do end at receptions, no one claps and urges them on, no one comes forward to cut in, no one dances next, a kind of triumph for the two of them.

They fetch their mother from the bathroom and find their way out of the place in the dark, pushing and jerking the wheelchair over gravel.

Three geese swoop down at the chair when they open the car door, *Christ* is what the elder says when she can't find the keys under the mat and her breasts pop out of her sheath, and the boy says nothing at all afterward, the best he can manage, this time saying it twice, his bride helping.

Burn the Bed

Tits on Candy, at least a 38. 5/4/83. Went with Fiona. 5/15/83. Nice you-know-what. June '83. A short one July 1, had to pick up the kid.

She shifts against the hot upholstery—she's heated it herself, with fury—and a blizzard of ancient plastic seat settles between the diary's pages so she can't read who he screwed in August. Or maybe a tear in her eye is the real problem. Not that she's crying. How lame to keep track of his dates of betrayal, how sad for him. Ha. All those nights he came home so late, with so little to say. He must have been tired.

All these little notebooks spill out of the locked glove compartment. She picks the lock herself—somebody at the upcoming estate sale will if she doesn't. He must have transferred them to every new vehicle he'd bought in the last three decades since they divorced, shoved them into Patty's van, then Tapestry's, who merely lived in. Patty and Tapestry probably didn't see the notebooks but maybe they did—Patty didn't answer the number she found on the internet to call, and Tapestry collected her toothbrush and vanished ten minutes after they drove up.

Her son inherited everything. Estranged as he was, she'd imagined he couldn't do the estate stuff alone and had volunteered to help. She had also imagined some satisfaction in the job, the good ole kiss-off. The first few days she'd had to figure out how to get rid of the body: the hospital, the funeral home, the cemetery. She might as well as have been scrubbing his toilet.

The windshield of the car she sits in is rock-pocked, the way she feels at the moment, hand on creepy diary: hit in the face by revelation. She wants to go on reading, and she doesn't. She stares across what passes for lawn in this part of the mountains: boulder, boulder, rags of weeds—and about a thousand antlers, scattered or piled around his shack, poking up in further weird rebuke.

Crying? says her son after tapping on the window. No, he doesn't say that, nobody says that, it would be too obvious—he must've said Frying? Her brain can't get around what is leaking out of her. He is holding up one of the many venison slabs they found frozen like so many accordion pleats inside his father's freezer. I found even more, he exclaims. A fucking feast.

She stops a last tear with the edge of the diary, its spiral binding nicking her eye, her ex's belongings continuing to get even. Tetanus for sure. She rolls the window down. I'll be just a minute.

At forty, he has curiosity, if not concern. What's with all the notebooks?

In her search for the dates that fell during their marriage, she has spread ten of them over the front seat and dash. He kept track of the mileage, she says.

Her son cocks his head at her as if taking aim. How did he learn to mimic her ex when she took him away so early? It means *Tell me the truth*, but she doesn't. She finds the plastic bag she'd been filling with debris and trashes every last one of the notebooks right then and there. They keep falling out of the bag or ripping at its flimsiness, shaming her in her panic to get rid of them.

I'll take it, he says, and sticks his hand over the sill and grabs for the bag.

She hesitates, she says, I'll put it out with whatever else I find.

You decide, he says, in that deadpan way her husband had. He shrugs. I'm doing dinner. He picks his way through the antler forest back toward the house, frozen meat in hand.

He loves her. He still lives in her house, he has abandonment issues. But she didn't abandon him, just his father. She left the guy not because he was cheating on her—she had no idea, well, no real inkling—but because of that deadpan way. Her ex couldn't have handed down abandonment issues, his parents didn't split up. What her ex did have was a slapdash fury that passed for passion in their brief courtship. She admired his certainty that she was his and in response, she marched down into her parents' basement and made herself a wedding dress in a single afternoon. No, it took a couple of days of sewing, but it seemed as if it were only an afternoon, it seemed as if she wore the finished dress up the stairs and kept on marching right down the aisle.

Cuckold, that is the word. What is the female equivalent?

They dine on venison stew concocted from frozen vegetables, wine vinegar, and bouillon cubes. Dining is too grand a term: taking the food out of circulation. They have already ransacked the house to secure less spoilage-prone valuables: the sleigh bed she so loved, for instance. Her ex, who never kept a job longer than a month and never had any money, liked old things with quality. Maybe she was quality? She hadn't been old when they split up, she had been too young to rent a truck to take the sleigh bed with her, too young to leave him sleeping on the floor. Besides, that deadpan look he had could explode into violence, that cocking head augured cocked fists—he was small and wiry like a boxer. She had imagined an explosion following her from the desert town she fled, her in the prow of a rented vehicle in the shape of the bent dark wood of the bed, beating horses forward through the brittle landscape.

They have almost finished dinner when her son lifts his knife a little too high. She doesn't imagine her son slashing at the scars at his wrists but his knife is indeed lifted, the wrist bent. She looks down at her plate, and is relieved to see from the corner of her eye that he goes back to sawing at his steak. The ex never tried to do himself in, he had a heart attack. In this one case, her son had opted to do something on his own. Of course it all has been her fault, even the heart attack of his father, even her son not getting a decent job, and maybe it was her fault he didn't bleed enough to die. He is saying now that he might move to New Orleans with Peter and the money from the sale of the house. It's pretty valuable.

She nods without changing her expression. Enthusiasm might cause him to change his mind. She can see him happy in New Orleans with his friend Peter, but she can't see him gay, the way she can't really see the diaries, their dates and names as evidence of his father's infidelity. But her son is already grizzled with a middle-aged manhood unfettered with child or wife. She loves him terribly anyway, even if he has other things she doesn't understand on his mind. He says he's decided to sell the house on his own. She should go home, send him his things. He'll live in the house until it closes.

With its knives and shotguns and tetanus-producing spiral bound notebooks that she sees have not yet made it to recycling? He'll occupy his suddenly dead father's last place of residence trying to reconnect with him in the silence and loneliness of this remote location? By himself and the scars on his wrists? You will not, she says.

When I got out of the service, he says in that deadpan way, sawing away, I thought I'd go into farming. Maybe I'll buy a pecan grove in Louisiana.

Pecans are expensive, she says.

Her new husband—after decades he is still new—hasn't allowed her enough money for a plane ticket home. They have separate accounts and she's never seen his. In exchange he pays for everything he approves of and that seldom includes her son. All these years, she alone took care of him, getting jobs teaching kids spelling, selling crafts that bloodied her fingers, and, in bad years, even babysitting to buy him new clothes. Now her son is rich, or will be, and it's not as if he has to pay her back, the way her husband insists.

The antlers are mine, she tells her son, the deer died here before you were born, and he doesn't protest when she sells them to raise money for her airfare. All the little dead Bambis are the women in the diaries, she decides, and she should get something out of that. Instead of flying, she rents a truck to drive the bed back. Her son can sleep on the pull-out couch in the living room while he sells the house. She drags the bottom bedstead out past the last of the antlers the morning she's leaving, her son sitting inside doing calculation after calculation about whether he should rent the house instead of sell it. She drags it over the rocks and burrs and sand-choked tags of plants down to where the car sits, trying to determine how to make it fit. She leans the bedstead against the door. Nice hard cherry. What a great bonfire it would make!

She returns to the house to find lighter fluid. She's sure she saw it somewhere in the drawer full of mismatched silverware but no, she'll have to go through one of the tins of old doorknobs and mini-wrenches and rusty nails, where he'd surely have stored it. She knows a few things from living with him. But instead of fighting her way through the trash in the basement and finding the tins, she takes a seat on the old rocker a room away from her son. She still can't believe what she found in the notebooks. By reading that stuff, she'd exposed herself to love's deadly radiation, as if she'd fallen asleep at the beach with all of her clothes off. Was she asleep beside every telltale date?

A humming noise. Like a horse, she picks up her head, she looks suspiciously at the corners and ceiling. She goes to stand at the center of the house and hears it loud. She's sensible: she does not scream. She tips her head, listening. What is this newer husband doing in their bed at home while she takes these two weeks to get rid of the old husband's body and sell all these antlers and maybe drive for days with this old bed in tow? Maybe she doesn't want to find the lighter fluid, maybe she has found something else, listening to this hum, a pattern?

She calls home and he doesn't answer. He said he was going bicycling as if he were on some kind of team. Maybe he is on a team and is screwing them one after another. She bets the bicycle remains untouched, unlike other things she might mention.

Sweetheart, she'll say when she turns up early, I can't spell en flagrante.

He will say Latin is not Italian. He went to Rome once without her, she has not forgotten, although it was years ago. When they arrived at the airport, his ticket let him on the plane, but not hers. Some mix-up in the reservations he made. He went anyway. Was there someone he met in that Latin-lover place, or someone with the right ticket, leaving from elsewhere? She hears that humming noise again, instead of his voice, the I-am-innocent sound that escapes his lips like a tune he can't quite carry.

Her son fills a pot for coffee in the kitchen. NPR is blasting away with its interviews that make people cry, with its sorrowful stock-market reports and variations-on-a-theme of housing crises, when her husband finally calls back.

It's really noisy here, he says.

She's supposed to guess where he is.

Niagara

The husband isn't breathing beside me, or else the bright snow
falling at that angle against the windshield forces his eyes closed—

A laziness derails my checking. Who wants to explain him being
dead all of a sudden, who wants to process it? He's not even ill. But
my laziness is born of generalized-looking-to-get-specific grief, like
an atom trying to make salt. I press the car forward, toward the
snow-slant, our destination crazy enough for such grief, a place a
river falls. Whatever skitters in the periphery could be getting specific
too, but I don't adjust the rear view to check.

Then it's *roar roar*. Car static caused by turning, or by following
this too-curvy road? Or the grief I've come to witness in the river
welling up already, or just pre-grief, some prep in nature, the cat-
aract practicing?

A pretzel's still tight in his hand, ready for biting. He bites it, says
he must've dozed off, what's that noise?

Tintinnabulation, I say.

He stops chewing, taps his working ear.

The car goes on into the roaring. I miss some ice. Deer make their
way roadside, one with a rack. I see its hoof tempted to lunge, then
I'm past him too, into more roar.

The white tail when they turn signals the others, he says. You
could probably see white like that in the dark, if you're a deer wanting sex.

Every seven minutes, I say.

Bambi, he says, giving me the sly eye.

He's definitely not dead. I'm getting hungry, I say. He hands me a pretzel. I bite bite bite. How long should we stay?

You mean should we just turn around and go home once we see it? Sensible, he laughs but let's wait-and-see.

He used to see me on weeknights and half Saturdays and fill my glass with wine in glugs I couldn't drink. Now he sees water in the basement and says I could be electrocuted.

Lots of other cars start thickening the roadway. There are lanes. Money will soon be given out at a window, exchanged for cold air.

The roar grows.

Have you ever seen a wonder of the world? I ask, to keep the grief off.

But he is asleep for real this time.

There's some fuss in the backseat, peripheral anxiety-provoking clamor I don't want to acknowledge. I press the automatic back window cleaner in proxy but can't help but look around. There are my two grown children whom I had not noticed in the car in their youth, now in a pose, elbows bent around their heads, talking into their phones. They are wearing sort of deer costumes—spotty with chips—as if changed into something more suitable for the outside-the-car weather, which has turned snow-feathery, with spray.

Maybe I stopped the car and picked them up.

My husband, awake again, hands around the bag of pretzels, all the way back to the backseat, and then there's a great sigh at the sighting of billboards, *At last*, like air escaping a tire. I park. It's the end of motion, which means there'll be emotion to follow, something electrical generating out of the flow and then stop.

But hey, no one cries—that's the upside of grown children. They will prance and gambol and suppress.

The husband is one second from taking off his seatbelt, he's ready already to put himself into line early. We can't even see the river from here but there's plenty of spray. Atomized, will it spray grief over everyone? is what I wonder but not aloud.

All of us are out of the car by then, even me, and the weeping of the scenery fits me fine.

It's not like I'm getting away.

He and the grown children are laughing at the bridal party drenched behind cameras and the cut out place to put your head in a hole.

My phone rings. *Don't answer it* runs between all of us, even the deer-in-headlights children, just don't, but its weird do-re-mi, its flash inside my pocket, its wriggle—I have to.

The grown children look into the distance with their new licenses, with their stocks and bonds, with their own portents. What I hear, I don't need to repeat, I stand there at the railing and look over it while they go for souvenirs. They buy them while I'm not repeating, then they go for food.

My husband slurps at his ice at the bottom of his drink. Here we are, he says after a while.

I order two of their best snacks and pocket the change. It could've been my heart, it is so heavy and cold and in so many pieces.

London Boy

It is almost midnight.

In search of cheer or drink or hail-well-met, the moon about to slide into the city, we are drawn past the windowpanes of pubs all the way to the river itself, the party inside those lit panes so seemingly private. The river is not lit, there is nothing party about it, which is a relief, and we hang over the railing and watch the moon catch on watery things.

She swam to a little island in the middle of the river, my husband is saying. After they'd stripped her and beaten her. Then they taunted her from the shore, offering her their coats.

It was a different river. I try to block my son's hearing by stepping in his way. At thirteen, his hearing is excellent.

An American river, says my husband. One of those cemented along the sides.

Was there a helicopter involved? asks my son, and throws a stick over the railing to show he's not really listening.

A heron falls into the dark river after the stick, dropping from the black sky through all the city light into our skein of gray gloaming.

None of us says anything, the way a crowd goes *Oh, my god!* without words. The bird wings itself up out of the darker water with no stick or fish or boot in its beak, which is no real surprise, given our mid-city locale, and the dark. It lands on its stick legs the length of that beak and preens a picturesque distance away.

What happened to the woman? I can't resist saying, three beats later. I should resist, for the boy's sake, but there's curiosity.

There was snow all over the island but she walked across it after it got dark, says my husband. Naked.

She'd curl up, says my son, hold her knees to her chest and stay low.

The heron holds itself as if drying its shiny beak in the electric light.

I am used to the bird by now, surely herons are always landing in London in the last hours of the year. I turn back to the river. She was menopausal, I say. She burned a path through the snow with her hot-flashing skin.

My son throws another stick. It goes along in the water, collecting foil and cups and fishing line.

The bird lifts itself into view right near our railing—bigger than I imagined, or is that just what it seems, so close and sudden? It flies or sort of dissolves back into the dark band along the banks. Could've been bunraku, I say. A Javanese shadow bird-puppet.

A solemn nod from my husband.

With the bird gone, we hear the traffic again behind us, the possibility of a bus. My son can't find any more sticks, he's eyeing the tree.

She actually waded across to the other side of the island and walked in the nude, in the dark, against the traffic on the interstate, says my husband.

We move to the curb and wait for the long light to start chirping Look Left. My son turns back to the railing, as if what we have seen will repeat itself. The light takes so long he turns around again and crosses with us.

She pounded on the door of the first house she came to, my husband has to say. Christmas lights blazing right up next to the busy highway, headlights on her buttocks.

You're elaborating, I say.

My son smiles at the two of us. Well, did they open up?

Not right away. The first house had a party going and couldn't hear her. Or so they said.

It would be hard to open the door to a cold naked frightened woman, I say.

While a block passes, I ask in the ensuing silence, Which way did the bird go?

It's just a story, says my son as we turn into a square. Nobody would really do that.

I read it, says my husband. Really, really, really. The second house had a gun.

Let's go stand on a bridge, I say. Where we can really see.

Brits sit in overcoats in the cold, drinking beer along the water's edge. Few of them look up when the first fireworks explode, where the smoke and theirs join, where you can still see "Pretty Girls" blink off and on a building. The bird isn't caught in the bursts of light, dazzled and taken down, as far as I can see. I stomp my feet to get warmer and say the night's over but the moon still hangs there so brightly it confuses even me.

Go on—shoot, says the drunken ten-year-old beside us, pointing his arm, taking aim at the sky.

That's the whole thing, says another. They did and just look at her now.

They didn't, did they? asks my son.

Kosciuszko Bridge

I sit abreast of the mother-in-law, tit dripping, baby logrolling thighs: mine, hers. Who makes up the rest of the crush? Your cousin, asleep, jaw hanging, seated on the far side of the mother, you, in heaven in the front seat, talking sweet about a film you hope to make to whomever beside you who also makes films, who says, Whoa! like that, in exclamation, when you stop, not short but ass-to-bumper-kissing, on the unpronounceable bridge. The truck driver behind us crushes gears, threatening to tap us too, then guns it, with hope.

Hope has been filling our car from baby-suck to the bent ears of all, even the sleeper who hopes no one noticed his snores, but especially the mother-in-law who avoids admitting she finds babies dull and disorderly, and instead casts out film-hope regarding you, she who has seen the city's skyline at the top of the bridge herself long ago and who also harbors the cocktail kind of hope.

All four lanes halt.

Like at the top of a Ferris wheel, I say with cheer. We are on the Up. Cheer is best for an in-law who has traveled the planet to find greeting-card images that a nonmilitaristic international organization is proud to feature children on. She is that kind of in-law, accomplished, and I am the other, except in the recent maternal. But her line of work suggests she likes at least pictures of children, and I've seen a distant don't-hug-me affection for you. She hasn't comprehended—her verb—grandchildren, but she is game enough. She touches her grandson's foot when he beats her leg in the ecstasy of milk-lust, she is sure he has her eyes. She is examining him now while I have him suspended by the underarms, head bobbing. The pre–baby seat era allowed that.

Some of the drivers beside us crack open their car doors. Try the radio, says the someone who is in film beside you in front and then he follows his own suggestion and tunes in—sports news—high pops from the outfield—temperature, almost cool enough to roll down the windows (we roll)—and national news.

Where are those traffic helicopters when you need them? you say, tapping on the windshield near its crack we hope your mother will notice and offer to fix.

I stick my head out the window and all that hope escapes. Someone many cars ahead cries.

The baby cries then too, drowning the other out, but we have all heard. I roll the window up again, the baby lunging for the opening, cry trailing.

An accident, says the film someone in front. Must be bad.

Those who have cracked their doors have already shut them, to keep the a.c. in, if not the crying out.

If it were an execution in the nineteenth century, crowds would gather, I say. I have a special knack for the dreadful.

My mother-in-law tells a very brief story about liberating Dachau. She has also worked as a journalist, she has heard cries. Is she competing with my dreadful?

The caught fly that no one has killed flies zzut, zzut behind the car visor and is now doing its hair with its legs, says the guy in front who brushes his hand at his own in the peculiar silence we make after Dachau, his hair film-ready like those in the industry who don't work that often.

In the car ahead swivels a plastic hula girl every time the rear passenger shifts to get a better look between his parents. Wide-eared, he must have heard the crying too, all their windows were down. His mother turns in her front seat and threatens him in word or deed, to sit still and he does, for three seconds.

I say, Somebody better check.

I don't say I have the hormones of life rushing through me, I can't help it, I want everything to live.

You get out, stretch, take off your sunglasses and toss them back into the car. This is no movie, says your cousin, blinking awake, vis-à-vis the guy in the front seat who doesn't budge.

I roll down the window again. I'd go, I say, but—

The baby dances in my lap in hidden agenda, like more milk.

Two cars ahead and I can't see you jog anymore, either you or your cousin.

My, my, says my mother-in-law. She says that word of possession whenever anything spins out of her control. I actually like her because she is so easy to assess: *my* not *your* telegraphed clear and direct. I've given up trying to convince her that I am more than a curious hanger-on with her son, that the marriage idea came from him, the gold to be dug being not readily apparent, the jewelry metaphor more diamond-in-the-rough.

The guy still in the front seat tries to talk more about films, a recital of titles someone her age might enjoy. She warms to him, but the crying outside is louder now since I feel it isn't right to roll up my window against it and I want to hear you, if necessary. The occupants of other cars have rolled theirs down again too, perhaps anxious and curious—what did we hear? One or two more follow you with mincing-in-between-the-car steps, but without cell phones because those electronics exist in a more driving-dangerous future than ours. Only green metal boxes with pictures of receivers embossed on their outsides allow stalled drivers access to 911 then.

This is not a stall, I say, out of the blue.

You are not there to tell me to stop being such a drama queen or to give me the eye that says the same without saying anything in front of your mother but it is you taking so long that makes me blurt this out. Disaster is catching, I say, the way women who are friends get pregnant, and I start talking about all the babies in our area that have come out of the woodwork, as if wood is some weird stork, and I stop.

No one is talking when you and your cousin's heads pop up over the horizon and now you are almost back at the car. The two of you carry the blank faces of shock, you especially who blanches even at the boo-boos the baby suffers, and such faces keep us quiet two beats after you get back in but it is me, always me, the baby pulling at my buttons after another milk session, who asks why you are missing your belt.

Tourniquet, you say.

We had to walk off the bridge to find a working phone, says your cousin. He opens his door again and tucks his head to vomit.

Lots of people there now, you say. No one then, you say.

We are returning from a visit to summer and its beaches. A story by Bradbury is in order: random cars gassed in the tunnel to the beach every weekend as a means of population control, but I don't tell it, nursing the baby to sleep at last, the kicking, very happy baby.

A person can't have too much blood, you say. You've gripped the wheel after your return as if it will fly up and hit you.

The baby belches and everyone laughs, we laugh weirdly and the baby cries, startled.

It's a sweet child, says my mother-in-law, the first plus-plus statement she's made all weekend.

You turn around, astonished. Mom, you say, you won't live forever.

You've rehearsed this line, it's supposed to be part of a private talk given while you return her to her airplane. There this opening line sits, the rest of the speech sorting itself out with the phrase "a few hundred dollars" foremost but unsaid at this time, with hope.

The cars move.

You have to be very careful, she says.

Is that my future too? I almost have the brains to wonder, with the baby finally sleeping, with an exhaustion no longer possible to contemplate.

The Stroke of Midnight

Imperious still, she sits propped in her bed set up on the patio surrounding the pool she built that forces a perspective of chlorinated water over the far edge, one that meets the ocean so without a seam you swim into it with your eyes, swim without the cliff that separates your perspective from one water to the next. Three of her sons watch the white glitter of the fireworks reflect that trick perspective, hear her lover bang at the door that he insists he owns half of, and drink a little wine. Because it is the New Year's fireworks, because their mother loves that holiday with its riot of resolutions and absurd abandon, they would've given her vodka through a tube if she had one.

But the tubes are gone, she only drinks sips of water.

The eldest calls from his family holiday. Not that she can talk to him. She had had to blink to affirm the document in which she decreed that starving was the way to go. One blink for no, two for yes, and repeated on numerous occasions thereafter. The eldest came up with this Morse code and tested her blinking even further, scientifically even, by asking if she loved him—two blinks—and whether he is the youngest, questions she can easily answer, blink! to establish a baseline.

The blinks have to be close together, not a blink, and then a blink.

The palms rustle. You can't have a woman in a sickbed outside on New Year's Eve in Hawai'i without palms. Palms rustle with geckos fleeing the sudden light of explosion, palms so far from where the eldest is spending his holiday without the grief given by this lover of hers who also put questions to her, the answers of which belie her clear mind, the blinking not right, not right at all, says the lover. Doesn't she love him more than her children? But she has changed that clear mind of hers at last and only blinked once. He had waited and waited for the next. Maybe what made a difference was all those two-timing years with that woman down the road who had so many facelifts her kept quality confused even him. It was their mother who kept him.

All those years the lover taunted the brothers, the eldest especially, the eldest who has to file the order to keep him from entering what he is claiming to be his own home that he swindled her out of so long ago. She was once his next-door neighbor but he had wooed her in widowhood, then she signed over those papers, giving him half of her house; she hadn't blinked then. They cannot keep him out under those legal circumstances of title and deed, and so instead they change locks and keep guard and sleep in shifts and file papers. Once he throws a brick through a window from his next-door lawn and sets off the electronic eyes and all the alarms. He also tries to cut off the ambulance with his car when they have her moved home, and finally he tries bribing the hospice workers, giving a diamond to the cute RN from the mainland with hot-pink lipstick, although they wonder how clear his motivations were with that one.

She has been dying for three weeks. Eating nothing and sipping water in a three-week torture for them suffered day after day, who redirect their grief to the lawyers who work for their fees with similar quotients of distress and hysteria. The eldest had terrible dreams while he waited with them, and then easily fell prey to his family's pleas to return for their holiday, if only for the presents. It won't be long now, his brothers keep telling him on the phone but it is, day after beautiful day.

Is it the lover shaking those palms? Is he, with benchpress determination, scaling their mutual wall and sliding down a palm? You can hear the rustling over the fireworks.

The second eldest does not flick on the wall light—he wants to see the fireworks explode star-bright, not to mention the constellations so strange at this dip at the equator. What is the equator for otherwise, other than another asset for their mother's fine real estate investment the lover covets? In the two hours before midnight all of them have spent getting a little high from the wine in the dark and quiet of their mother's outdoor bedside, not even eating, no, not even the youngest, the burliest, eats in her presence to validate her decision, and even the clouds have held themselves off while the bay slides over the side of the equator the way the pool water does to the bay, that pool now so full of stars and so soon explosions.

The youngest engineers a toast a few moments before midnight, before the sprays of light and the booming obliterate all sound. For kindness and mercy. Hear, hear, shout the others, hoping she can hear, that her single blink and then another five minutes later signifies two this time and forever. Then the eldest calls and cries on the phone. He remains torn at his nonequatorial home and there, though the third son takes the phone to reassure him his mother is holding up, doing as well as can be expected, is still good, and he doesn't hang up, he leaves the phone on the tray table where his brother can hear the fireworks at least, their cheers and their glasses coming together and the palms rustling so loudly that when all the fireworks end, in one long exhalation of explosion and brightness, their mother all lit up like a sudden tropical sunrise, her eyes filled with light, so even he hears the lover's enraged *Murderers!*

An octogenarian Tarzan, a desperate and furious and still virile and hirsute suitor, he bellows and flashlights them, having scaled the wall with a ladder on his side and a rope on the other and that is when the third son notices, in that post-explosion stunned light and fury, that their mother isn't blinking, that her stare has slipped over the pool's edge into the ocean.

But the lover is busy. Is it a kiss he is after by ignoring the restraining order? A simple *Happy New Year's, honey?* He swings the flashlight at the brothers, a big one. Although the second son soon has him stopped, it is not without the old man blackening the eye of the middle one who, about to pour a new bottle of wine, finds it awkward to dodge him. The fourth son might have shouted *You're too late* just then in a kind of victory but doesn't, he is lifting the mother's hand over the other.

They forget the eldest in all that and what they do after. At dawn a housekeeper replaces the receiver.

The Red and Purple Blooms

Even prone she looks angry: the jut of her hip against the bed, her eyes slipping around their sockets in fury, her fingers claws. She flinches when she's offered a forkful of her favorite, volcano cake, as if it were an affront. You think you're going to buy me off? Cordial, she isn't. Is she in pain? No, never, she says through clenched teeth and hands.

She has a mane, still black and thick, that spreads over her pillows, but all the hair has fallen off her legs, limbs in the past stubbled with black-razored stumps. Overhead, the TV is always on, tipped to match the angle of her bed, and turned up so she doesn't have to wear hearing aids, or because that way she can't hear anyone else over the Fox confirmations of her anger. Head of the state's anti-abortionists, she knows her leanings. Women should die if they try to kill their children.

I say some people are irresponsible at that time of their lives, and someone has to take care of all those unwanted children. She says now and before that she wouldn't have had any of the nine of us, but for our father.

He stands around. He isn't what he calls a sucker for punishment but he doesn't divorce her. Too late, he says, as if those prior decades he considered too early, when he might have missed all that sex. Besides, she believes in the forever of marriage, it is another edict of the Catholic church she chooses to swallow.

She opens her mouth like a bird in my direction but I don't notice, I am captivated by a tell-all interview spewing from her screen. She mutters, assuming I cannot hear her over the noise, she says I will write a tell-all about her.

As I shovel the cake into her, I think no, I won't.

But I can always reconsider.

Over the five years of her bedridden glory, the doctor diagnoses nothing. Can you die of hate? My siblings and I want to know if it's catching, if there are genes to suppress. The flowers of our youth play video games at home, the noise of which we know to be even louder than this TV, the hospice nurse calling for morphine, my father dealing another hand of solitaire while the chatty, scantily clad assistant rubs his back. A little lower. We vow these children should not have to endure the same excruciating pageant. We think pills for ourselves or gas ovens, given the family predilection for long lives, but nobody asks for prescriptions, everyone buys electric.

She wants to push us into the oven of her anger, I tell my sister. She wants to eat us to stay alive.

Our very presence annoys her, says my sister.

Behind those sugar-paned windows of childhood, we never argued with each other, we linked arms when we could. Now we buy stinky cheese that she doesn't spit out, swathed on a cracker whose shards might just kill her, we thaw more chocolate cake from a freezer full of it. We speak on the phone to those at home, failing to convey the horror of her dying, conveying only that spring is coming, and the bulbs we planted in the fall will soon force themselves past the ice and into red and purple blooms of bouquets we will bring her by the armful.

Surely she will have a change of heart and love us. In the hour before she dies, she reiterates why she will leave us nothing. Each of us have only a few children, which means surely we have had abortions. It is obvious, never mind our protests. What she loves instead of us are the clothes in her closet. Her many dresses do not need hangers they are so crushed against each other. Ostrich bags, mink hats. Soon after she expires we take turns picking from the loot, packing each item carefully, but as soon as we arrive home we throw them out or hustle them off to Goodwill, although one sister hangs a few choice suits on the wall as if mounting Mother.

The bulbs we anticipated, their red and purple blooms so like bruises, have not appeared by the time we pack up. Perhaps they will not. Perhaps they have been planted too deep, and the ground we thought would protect them will turn out to have been too dark and too heavy.

The Bulkhead

The dog was a new and full-out puppy, a licker of face—and air if he lacked a human cheek. He took the road off leash, bounding forward, a small creature with a squirrel tail heedless of destination, all exploration. The beach offered a runway: he zoomed across the sandy strip, ignoring the osprey swooping with interest, he ran right to the end of the beach and leapt over the bulkhead and dropped five feet into the inlet.

She had been larking along behind him, oblivious to the possibility that a puppy wouldn't know to stop. She ran to the bulkhead as fast as she could, unbelieving, and seeing no other exit, looked down. He was swimming for the first time in his life close to a current that could pull him out to sea. She threw herself over the bulkhead and down its rough face to a ledge just over the water, and leaned out, extending her hand.

Dogs do not grasp, dogs paddle, all legs rotating. However far she stretched was moot anyway, there was too much distance between them already. She skinnied back up the side, shouting encouragement like *Hold on! Keep it up!* and scanned the beach for a broom handle, or something broom-handle-like. That survey of beach grass took about a second before she called it off, not to mention the above problem of opposable digits. She knew the current, when he hit it, would be lethal. Oh, where was her husband, quick-thinking with regard to all things water? A ten-minute walk, a whole forever.

She ran to the adjacent parking lot.

One car.

She ran to the car.

On the opposite side, two folding chairs, two people apparently not big on the beach. She pleaded anyway: My dog fell in the water! She was still hoping for a broom-like something, the windshield wiper or antenna-to-spare and circled the car. By the time she made it around, the man, bearded, in shorts and now not wearing a watch— throwing it down with his sunglasses—raced back to the beach with her at his heels. Okay, he said, where she pointed, panting, hardly able to keep up.

The dog's head was still visible. The current beckoned, swirling him left and right.

The man stripped off his shirt and dove in.

She knew it was cold; it was definitely wet, it wasn't his dog. People are always jumping in and then drowning instead of rescuing someone or thing—but he saved him, hauling the dog to the embankment where she grabbed him by the collar, the rest of him too slippery that wet. She hugged his wet fur and he licked her face. The man launched himself out of the water to the ledge, and over, teetered for a second as if he weren't quite strong enough to pull himself up, and climbed out.

What to say after? Just thank you? What's your life history, how do you happen to have these generous and athletic reflexes? How can I ever repay you?

He screwed his dry shirt over his wet chest. She dug the leash out of her pocket, the dog shook the wet all over her while she clipped it on. Thank you, she said.

He didn't say what an idiot she was to let the dog run, he said, The dog might vomit up salt water.

You are my hero, she said next as they walked back to his chair on the tarmac and his girlfriend standing beside it, holding the abandoned drink. Is this a habit?

They laughed.

The dog shook himself again, the cold water must've soaked deep, and pulled on the leash to go farther, its near-drowning a drama of five minutes.

Watching such unfold was only for a moment frightening. It wasn't in the watching either, that's panic, or in the rescue, which is relief, the plain effort of understanding what happened. She wasn't shaking now. Had the dog learned anything about the beach's boundaries? She didn't test him.

About a month later, she saw the rescuer on the tarmac again, his beach chair deployed this time in a circle of ten or so mostly men. He was speaking to them as she and the dog crossed the lot. She couldn't hear what he was saying, then he stopped and some other man spoke from his chair.

She got closer, wanting to thank him again, but he wouldn't look at her or the dog. They were discussing how to detach with love. Did the meeting have something to do with alcohol, either quitting it or surviving someone else's habit? He might have had to rescue himself a thousand times.

They walked on. At the beach, the dog stared at her with pleading eyes. The waves, she told him, would drown her faster than him. He whined. No, she said. She circled around and found the rescuer packing up from the meeting. Before she could say anything, he said, folding his chair, you have to let a dog run. Then wait for the splash.

What she wanted to tell him was that her thirty-year-old son's doctor said he'd need a new liver if he didn't stop drinking, so her son ordered a case of Beaujolais to celebrate. Instead, she said the dog needed his leash, and walked home.

Where Fatherhood Goes Bad

A real bonfire. A log, two logs, three, not kindling, a blaze roaring over the water lapping the pier, a place of red eyes in the dark, and crashing flaming collapse.

Men who are willing to think themselves boys stand around as if the fire can fix them, their hands hanging confused, deprived of hangers skewered with marshmallows, and these men cry. Men like him, haggard with stuff men don't want other men to know about.

Robocop, the obvious name for the guy weeping beside him, hammer-fists tight with the tattoo of a snake coiled over knuckles triple-sized because he can't help but pop them—Robocop smiles but the tears rolling across his grim lips make him look half-drowned. *Mom*, he screams and pops those knuckles.

So what, he's screaming too, he's crying.

Third hour, maybe 1:30 a.m., the facilitator hands out sodas. A lot of the guys have acted out, he's seen bludgeoning: log against log, plenty of pretend sex-throttled agony, one guy off in the dark tearing his clothes to shreds, screaming *Too late*.

A note in his head goes off with that particular scream. Instead of putting the vision of his parents' friend, Mr. Roeser, the radio announcer/newspaper photographer and all-around Eagle Scout pressing him hard against the wall, Roeser's hand on his back so he can't move and his other hand unzipping over and over, the Ping-Pong ball bouncing in the background, a TV cartoon trying to end— instead of that, the primary reason his shrink says, Go to this weird bonfire event—he imagines his brother taunting him la-la-la as if he knows about Roeser, using that la-la-la to inform his father that he thinks he's of another persuasion because he said no to his and his dad's deal, and a particularly red thick log rolls in the fire in front of him. *It's not too late.* He heaves that log out of the ashes, burning his hands, and throws it, sizzling, into the waves.

The deal his brother and his father wanted him to be part of, the crops grown and sold so as to screw his sisters out of their share and keep all government money is what he'd said no to, It's wrong and I'm not going to do it. Your honor, he said to his dad who was once a judge and knew which way the loopholes looped. His brother laughed and his dad frowned and said, It's not too late, and when he said, Sorry, his dad pushed him away, the pressure of his touch just like Roeser's against the wall, a man who'd had a drink with Dad and Mom nearly every week of his growing up—*Hi, guys.*

Robocop catches him spitting into his blistered hands like somebody with asbestos fingers, trying to wrestle another burning log out of the embers, and helps him maneuver the unburnt end of it into the ocean, cursing and crying. They pummel the sand afterward, then he and Robocop and five others take the rest of the bonfire apart and call it quits.

He fills with happiness when the car starts the way a car might not after sitting in the sand for all those dark damp hours. Starts right up.

He is driving Dad home those many years ago, even before the deal, with a little detour past his very-own-bought-just-this-year field. Or is it an accident, a path that Dad would have avoided had he been driving? He looks out on the bent dry cornstalks, the first ones he'd grown all by himself instead of going to art school. Put that money you saved up into the ground and it'll come right up again bigger, said Dad, when he was in high goad-mode.

What does he see in amongst those cornstalks now? Cattle, devouring them. He slows, the dust catches up, the cattle wander off. I didn't rent that out for them to eat, he says. Did they jump the fence from your place?

Dad is smiling. He says, smiling, They're McCormick's cows.

They're just about past the field, he could just forget what he saw, he could just drive on. Well, what are McCormick's cows doing eating my forage?

I made the deal, says Dad. I keep the money.

He's so shocked he doesn't stop, he keeps on driving down that dusty unpaved road, the hot late sun at the end of it. They're another two miles before Dad says: You're a young farmer. You've got a lot to learn.

That year's revenues he didn't plant, they went straight into tuition.

The very same night when he gets home from the fires, shaking sand all over the foyer, leaving his sandy shoes under the bench and tiptoeing into the kitchen, he still has something else he has to do. Unfortunate scheduling but he'd already paid the money on both. He smells smoke and checks the kitchen where his worried wife waits, who whispers, How'd it go? That's when he realizes the smoke is himself, he stinks of it, but nonetheless gives her a kiss and goes to shower, puts on unguent, and finds a change of clothes. It's now 3 a.m.

Still damp, he enters his daughter's bedroom. This time of night she's usually at the junior high parking lot checking out porn online or perusing the dark web because they've blocked her, the junior high providing reception for the very poor or, in her case, the deprived recalcitrant defiant adolescent she has grown into. Now she lies in bed with her eyes closed, Sleeping Beauty at seventeen, and not the witch, snarling because he caught her getting a picture of his credit card while he was on the phone and had to change the number before he left. Thank god her friends cavorted in her room all day, doing what? he wonders, and wore her out. Maybe. He can't tell if she's really asleep.

He stands there for a good ten minutes until he hears his wife answer the door downstairs, the clock fall off his younger daughter's bureau in the next room, the couple they've hired cough just outside the bedroom door before they enter. The door opens, his younger daughter, night-clad, flits across the hall to the bathroom just as his wife and the couple burst in, and she sits up in bed.

I'm not a bad father, he says over her screaming. His wife tries to hold her daughter's hand to calm her. She believes in touch like religion, being an acupuncturist, but her hand hits the clipboard out of the man's grip after he announces, You're going away, and she starts to sob.

His daughter's out of bed quick, she says she's going to the bathroom but not alone, oh no, the woman has to go with her. There are razors in there. This caution is what you pay for. More tears—not his daughter's, mind you—but his, trying to stuff her backpack with t-shirts and socks. His wife stands frozen beside the bed. Get the fuck away, his daughter is yelling at the woman inside the bathroom.

I'm going to hold your arm behind your back when I walk you to the car, says the man just the way he said it so quietly in the salesroom —really the shrink's office—where they had come to the very very end of their rope, coiled at their feet the way they had found the knotted torn sheets left in front of the house one morning, her still stoned and drunk asprawl behind a bush where she'd fallen, stolen silver in her purse along with vomit.

He focuses on the word *hold*, which is what as a father he'd done: she was in his arms straight after her bloody birth, touching his silly beard, the hip one. When she'd fallen over a toy she'd wrenched from a playmate and cut her lip, he'd held her then too, he'd held her while the first shrink refused to take them on as a family, who said it was her problem, not theirs. Untrue, untrue, was his response. They would get through it together. They had tried everything, so many more therapists, family groups, zoom meetings, and, more and more often, legal actions. His wife had a mother who'd behaved the same way and ended up homeless. I'm crushed, says his wife, between my mother and my daughter. He adored his wife, a red-headed wisp of strong words and such a soft touch.

The man and the woman take his child away and drive to the wilderness where she will camp and survive. For three months. Nothing about them or their exit is left in his head by the time he and his wife go walking down the middle of the street to the shrubbery thin around the parking lot of the junior high where their steps stop, where they'd found her so often when she wasn't returned home by police car, and they cry and hold each other, then part when their younger daughter says, hiding in her pjs in the shadow of the all-carved-up *I love you tree* at the end of the lot, I'm hungry.

How is it that these people we're related to cause such chaos, is not what he will say in the deposition he will give against his father the very next week.

His lawyer primes him fifteen minutes before the hearing to say only yes or no. *Would you care to elaborate?* is a trap.

Did your brother unduly influence your father to sign all these papers? asks the other side.

Yes, he says.

Did your father have dementia?

Yes, he says.

Would you care to elaborate?

My father had intermittent dementia.

They should have talked about his brother who is not the least intermittent, he is determined to take everything. He does say his brother had already taken his father's home for himself and put him in assisted living and left him there over the holidays.

Then he stops. *I don't know* he remembers his lawyer saying is an answer that makes you less responsible.

Roeser presses hard against him, silent, rubbing rubbing rubbing.

I don't know, he says over and over.

What about this statue? asks his sister.

They have a very short time to choose who's going to immortalize Dad. He left money to the library that has to put up whatever bronze they pick. *Left* is not exactly it. The library mocked up a picture of a library with his name across it. When he didn't die fast enough, they put someone else's name on the library, but kept his money. The statue is a sop.

He mulls the bronze farmer, ball cap low, bronze fingers gripping his thighs as if he is about to spring up and drive a tractor for ten hours.

Or these abstract ones? asks his sister, one I-beam balanced on another.

Out of art school now three decades, he still knows how objects speak for themselves. I like the abstract because anybody can attribute anything to it, he says, but realism gives whoever the opportunity to go ugly and there Dad'll be, for the whole town to see.

Bronze just the middle finger? His sister has her own agenda. Maybe we could have his face emerging from the bronze, half-smothered, just his nose and eyes, a compromise between abstract and figurative and dead.

Compromise, he says, is not an aesthetic solution.

Okay, shut your eyes and pick one.

He does. It's one of the casserole artists, who favors features, he says, that resemble the rubble of cooked vegetables.

You don't ever have to visit, she says. They can put it in a glass case and shove it behind the shelves like they do the founder's.

In that case, let's make it as big as possible—how much bronze can you get for $50,000? We'll pour it down a wall through a lost wax mold and voila: a mess. Why not?

You're the youngest, Dad adored you, she says. We were all jealous.

He breaks down and tells her about his cornstalks. She registers little surprise. The youngest wasn't favored, that's all I'm saying, he says. I guess I did what I liked under the cover of jealousy. We should pick something that turns green. How about making it in copper?

You're forgiven, she says.

He opens his hands to see how the blisters are doing.

Silent Night

All is calm, all is bright—
　　What's so calm around here? I interrupt.
　　Sibling Three stops with the piano. Shshshsh. Dad.
　　He looks asleep in his chair.
　　Maybe you think he didn't notice? I say. What's it been—twenty-four hours?
　　Dad bats his faked-closed eyes. Okay, Mom took off. My fault. He closes them.
　　Sibling Four asks if anyone knows how much gas she had.
　　As if that is the determining factor, I say. I'm in a huff. She could have taken a plane to Paris by now, for godsake.
　　Have some eggnog, says Dad, sitting up. I liked the singing. Sing more.
　　We sing. A whole goddamn songbook of songs. We are trailing off with la-la-las when the phone rings.
　　Dad waves his hand from his chair in an OK, you get it.
　　Siblings Four and Five toss Who me? to each other while it goes on ringing, but of course, I answer.
　　The eldest, I say.
　　Wrong number, says the voice. The second after the click, I know. Let's not answer next time, I say. Let's let her stew.
　　Dad opens his mouth.
　　When do we open the presents? says someone small in mixed-up pajama feet.

Soon, says a sister, to whom he belongs. The PJed one creeps over to sit in Dad's lap but he's got his head in his V-ed hands, like a choice morsel being offered up. What can he do to get her back? He used to bring home a dozen roses wrapped in tissue. But here we are again, three short of a dozen, having ourselves flown in for the holiday. Maybe we are what she has flown from. The whole role.

Light the candles, says Dad.

Their dappling seems anxious, all the serenity skipped or shorn. There's a broken wooden lamb under the glass table some baby has teethed on we all stare at, the lamb's eyes so pocked and tooth-hammered Sibling Two says, Maybe Mom can see us.

That's the guardian-angel take, says Sibling Three while his kid cries *Mine!* over the lamb. Doesn't fit. The angel part, the guardian part—Mom has never played it. Maybe a hologram you could put your hand through.

She could have driven too fast and be dead and that's why she hasn't called again, says Sibling Eight. And then she could see us.

We all look into middle distance where TV static forms but there's no answering that, no solace like, say, calling the police. No one even suggests that.

What about an ad in the back of the newspaper? A poster on a pole?

She never slows down, I say.

What about leaving a note for Santa to look for her? asks one of the kids.

We decide for the children's sake not to talk about it. Instead we chew our fingernails shorter, we read the same bedtime stories twice, we don't open the presents. We think we should wait for her—until the kids show us what they think. They tear strips from the thinner-wrapped packages, crash their airplanes into the plush ones, and poke at the boxes with scissors until it's nobody's fault, not really. The gifts escape, that's what the eldest of them says.

I always liked the eldest.

The phone does ring again. We are half-relaxed or feigning it so just anyone answers. It's for you, Dad, is just as casual. We lean toward each other so as not to seem any more interested than anyone else; we nod, to a man, with our slight dissembling.

Someone's child panics with wrapping paper stuck to her thumb so we don't hear any actual words.

Dad takes to the couch afterward to give the orders: every room picked up, thank-you notes pinned to the presents, and a lot of puckering. Dad doesn't tell us anything really, other than *Soon*. He closes his eyes.

Soon is three days more, practically a Christian miracle. She is in the door before any barked alert. Bologna has just dropped from my sandwich so I have an ear to the floor, retrieving the meat when she shakes off her boots in the hall. Then the door to their bedroom eases itself closed, the one I once stood and pounded against all one Sunday siesta.

I am, like, cool.

I rush downstairs where a large percentage of siblings have unfolded sleeping bags or inflated "temporary solutions." Since it's getting dark, the glow of bad TV on their skin is festive and it gets downright cheery after I tell them the news. For a while.

So? says Sibling Two. I came all the way from Chicago. She can come down the stairs and see me.

I'm afraid to go up, says Sibling Seven, almost the baby. What if she leaves again?

You wish, says the baby.

She's found something under the sink to bang, says Sibling Three with an ear to the pipes.

We drift up the stairs. Dad nods as if our very existence is a surprise to him. With all of our courage gathered, so silent, so kind of casual you'd think all we saw was a deer standing there stopped at the window, and not her, now drinking a glass of water.

Someone sneezes like *Excuse me*, and she turns to face us. Sibling after sibling looks down the corridor behind her as if it hides something they can't wait to find.

She says to us all, Where's your baby? in such a tone that even I forget I haven't had one for years and go look.

Cozy Island

I must have telephoned him. It had been well over a year since I'd seen him, but he didn't say no to my visit when we talked, despite Kate. I hadn't known about her, I hadn't known until decades later, reading his bio online, that he had just returned from North Africa. I'd just returned from Sudan.

I must not have given him a chance to tell me. I must have telephoned him and heard a muffled yes from between his bearded lips. Kate must have had a day or two to prepare. Were they just living together? When I arrived, she stood behind him—loomed is what comes to mind—while he took his pipe out of his mouth and smiled at the boy who had wriggled out of my arms to stand.

The driver of the car opened her door to chat. She had been silent with me, wary, like any islander would be with strangers who'd begged for a ride at the ferry. She asked Kate if she had oysters, would she take two bunches of lettuce for a dozen every week if they decided to plant. The weather will be complicated after June, said the driver, eyeing my child and my big smile so obviously more about arriving than *Thanks for the lift*.

Nothing was decided, but Kate said she would look after the woman's dog while she went off-island. She was suffering from cabin fever, a condition, he said after she drove away, that besets everyone here after a while.

The island had a fever. I remembered that well.

Did we have tea? The climate was wet and cold—good for lettuce—and tea fixes the cold, said Kate, steering whatever must be said in her direction, and a kind of tea-stalling would have gone on, and dry cookies—biscuits—would have been found for the boy to gnaw, honey for the hot tea, a clearing-of-throat by him as if a speech were to be given, despite the pipe. How long will you stay? was the important question. Why are you here? would have been second.

Seven hours it took to come here from the mainland, traveling two ferries, and then hitchhiking between, and at the end. The sun would soon be setting. He had another friend who would put me up, no bother, she was always glad to have someone in the house, especially a child. He made the call, then put out his hand toward my boy. He did not ask after the father. His own, he said, had started boarding school on the mainland near his mother. The drugs on this island!

He was no child-lover. You could ascribe a certain fatherliness in his gesture but I knew the caring and feeding was beyond him, it occurred in a cloud in which another sex struggled. Years ago I'd amused his boy while he painted. The boy had to be kept from wandering too far from the house, was often underdressed and furiously demanding when hungry. Now, with mine, I understood a little better the complexity of this child-love being in competition with what he might have felt for me, and doubly overwhelming for someone wanting to make art.

Art would have been the subject at tea. Kate made art too, in many media, although her efforts weren't as inspected or respected as much as his, but whether the resin in his resin-cast paintings was all that held his workshop together was a hard call after a look into his lean-to studio.

Soon after tea, I began to shake with the chill. My friend said he would drive me to the woman with a spare room. En route I couldn't stop telling him how difficult my adventures in Sudan had been, the boy being the final result, and I talked on in the dark house for an hour about my confusion between adventure and abuse, shaking, sitting on the bed of the tiny backroom where his friend had put me. His pipe lit the space. Was he giving off empathy? I told him how it reminded me of the embers that little girls blew on while they ran to the next hut to make a new fire.

My boy was asleep in my arms, off what schedule he had, lulled by all my talk. After another half hour, he said Kate was waiting for him, that we would have dinner the next night at another friend's place.

Kate won't cook for another woman, he said. Unless she sleeps with them.

Was that a dare?

Could be, he said.

He had spoken of sex. I wondered then if I were to lay the boy on the bed and remove my dusty pants and shirt, whether we should take up again, but he sucked on his pipe once more, and said goodnight.

The boy and I ran down the beach all morning in that silent way you do when one of you is still mostly animal and the other is completely inside her head. He cut his hand and I found a Band-Aid, he was hungry and I gave him a piece of toast saved from breakfast. My hostess, a cheerful woman who spent the meal on the phone, left to go weaving up-island and told me to lock up.

Sometimes I ran too far down the beach, and the boy couldn't keep up, and cried. We made a teepee out of the lighter flotsam and sat under it at noon, cooking sand pies and moving stones into patterns of nearly the same swirl we had found them in. The child hadn't been witness to my adventures and certainly wouldn't have understood why I needed to tell this man every detail of it I could remember. I didn't understand either, except that I craved to have someone not dismiss what had happened, or block it with envy. I sensed Kate had an acute case of envy, although only about my time with him. He was still attractive and she hadn't been living with him when I'd left not so long ago on my adventure.

The two of them picked us up for dinner, the boy in his last clean pair of pants and me in a silk skirt that flowed when I walked, with a little drama, but we needn't have dressed. Wearing a pair of dingy shorts and no shirt, he went off to his friends' down the road, and I was left behind with Kate to prepare something—a salad, or snap beans? This abandonment had been planned. He said we could talk and then walk down the road to dinner whenever we felt so moved.

I set to whatever task I was assigned while keeping an eye on the boy running too close to the cliff that the house stood on or rather, nearly toppled from. My friend had been shoring it up from below, one log at a time, but it had rained hard for six months, and had rained every year before, and the shoring left the house at an angle that Kate explained could easily be fixed if he only sold one more painting.

I knew about such precarity, and wondered about its effect on someone who relied so heavily on selling someone else's painting, but I asked instead about the paintings of the man who was giving us dinner. I knew few neighbors from my time on the island.

He owns the paint, she said. His father's business, good for houses, and the quantity the son could get made him famous for big efforts in abstraction. She hadn't mentioned the woman who appeared at the door just then with a pot that she'd borrowed, partner of the abstract painter, the pot an excuse to scrutinize me in advance. Or did the two women have more of a plan?

I need to borrow your big knife, said the woman after the pot was returned to its cupboard.

I was changing the boy's shirt, sticky with something he'd found on the floor, I didn't watch as the knife came out of the drawer and went into her hand, nor any nonverbal exchange.

And that extra bottle of gin he said you had.

Extra? laughed Kate. She poured out drinks for us, settling most of the ice in my glass. As the freezer was tiny I felt honored, and was soon gin-happy regardless of my ration. Watch for the thorns, Kate cautioned as we set off to walk the mile or so down the path, carrying our drinks high, and the big knife in the other woman's hand. Every few feet another bramble, or the smooth limbs of arbutus against the sun and the water, or my son stretching out his hand to catch at the softer ferns. Only once, confused about which way to go, did I look up from navigating the path to see the woman a long way ahead with her knife raised in a gesture toward me, and was that Kate agreeing?

I fell further behind, the boy wanting to be carried. He couldn't walk the whole way, his legs were too short and his interest too fleeting to stick to the path. I held him close, and the dark was soon close too. I lost sight of both women but I never considered giving up. Dinner was at stake for my son. I hoisted the boy to my shoulders and he was floppy, nearly asleep, by the time I found the right turning.

Did they go out to find me? Did they call out my name?

The paint manufacturer's son offered new drinks all around when I turned up—*To the island!*—and then gave us plates of cooled food. He had heard something about my travels, who doesn't love an adventurer? he said. I smiled wide enough, and looked out into the dark rather than comment.

The studio stank of turpentine and the unfinished business of painting. The women were talking about what size canvas made sense in this weather with all the warping, the men were moved to consider paint chips by referring not to the names but to paint numbers. Another round of drinks. Our host asked: Did I want one of them to drive me back to where I was staying? The girlfriend said she was sober, grabbing onto the tabletop as if it were the one swaying.

I could've stayed there and curled up with my son who was sleeping on a pile of painty plastic drops near my stool. Or I could've asked my friend to walk me back to his house and use his car to return me. By then he'd be clear-headed—I remembered his quick way with liquor. In the quiet that opened up between the girlfriend's invitation and my hesitation, I said Sudan hadn't the cloud cover of here, and it was never so dark.

And you always knew where you were by the stars, he said, removing the pipe from his mouth.

I had told him too much.

Kate drove me back instead. There had been a fuss walking home when he couldn't find the keys, and then she did. After a mile or two she told me about the knitting project she'd started. She planned to knit a cozy for their car to protect it during the winter. And then she would knit one for the house.

I got the message.

On the ferry I tried to have my son wave at the woman we'd stayed with but by the time I'd hoisted him to the railing she had already driven off. Balling his fists to his face and yawning, he told me he heard bears all night. They walk around in the dark, he said. The black that were the firs we left behind was soon gray in the rain, a drizzle so light it stayed in the air and we breathed it in, like something that couldn't be told.

Camp beside Water

It was the second set of tenants, the wife who was the physical trainer, I tell my big son. The husband who gave you his shirts.

Yeah? he says. The people who left with the baby?

I bring over a new log because the fire has dwindled to the light of my son's device. I'm sure it wasn't his, I say.

How do you know, my nosy mother? says my second son, hot-dogging a stick.

I don't answer right away, I listen for the ocean, it's out there, hot blank swipes at the beach near people luckier than us in tent location. Only once did he leave for the weekend, I say.

Give it up, says my husband. What kind of spooky story is this? He's already on to the marshmallows, he's thumbing one off to my big son.

Don't interrupt, says my second son. I'm wondering how she knows.

Nine months before, a guy rang the bell at 3 a.m. that weekend he was gone. I remember. I let him in.

You walk in your sleep, that's what I know, says my big son who did catch me once at a mirror in France when jetlag played a part.

The guy was drunk, she's right, says my husband, I woke up too, I heard him. Oh, sorry, says my husband, sitting on the big son's device, but it is fine, it's still making its noise.

Morality isn't everything, says my second son while the marsh-mallow flames. Tweet that, he says to his brother.

None of you saw the woman, blowsy, tipsy, calling the guy her cousin for my benefit.

Her husband was nice, that tenant, says my husband. Give him a break. And put that down, he says to my big son about his device.

The wind blows ash over the food, the mustard tips over. My big son's already not sleeping in the tent but in the car, he didn't bring a toothbrush, let alone a bag. He keeps his device on.

My second son asks if the baby looked like him.

It only had to look like her, says my big son, thumbing again.

My husband covers the fire although there's still wood to burn. The next campsite is raucous with family, no devices there. But the big son can't not check, he checks. It's like a firefly, it's like one of us is not beside a beach surrounded by beauty but sitting in the dirt in the dark.

The tenant will never know. I didn't tell.

Years from now, he'll knock on our door, says the second son. I lost something here, he'll say. But you won't help him.

I'll be a hero, I say, wrapping the hotdogs. And say nothing again.

My girlfriend's sister is lost, says my big son slowly. The police are looking for her. They haven't found her but they think they know where she's hiding. He stands up as if he's crossing the 3,000 miles to instruct them, he takes a step toward the car where our picnic is poised.

At least they don't think she's dead, says my husband.

He shrugs and opens a container on the hood. She's probably pregnant.

Hope it's not yours, says his brother.

Like rabbit parents, we swivel our heads. What?

Just kidding, he says, Cool Whipping his brother from a container who pretend-shaves the foam off and eats it. Want to swim? he says. It's probably dangerous.

Our sons take off for the water, the dark barely glowing campsite behind them, the device part of that glow left behind on the hood of the car.

My husband castanets his sticky fingers together and says, They both look like you.

Good, I say, and I dance closer.

Orphan Shop

Ditziness, a kind of Morse code of shriek-and-stop, erupts around the girls—whoever heard of a guy in the ditzy department?—until they halt, one, two, three, each bumping into the other, at the orphan shop.

Adoption's fun, says the front one.

You'd think we didn't have fun, says the next, the way you say that.

The front one demurs, forcing the third into talking: Halves are the way to go, half-sisters, that way you stay out of the shops, you've got what you want, a relative relative, just a little.

Two orphans not a lot younger than the girls, press themselves against the window, making sad weather for the girls grouped outside, who mouth *Orphans* like a hit song.

I've heard of baskets of them left behind, where you don't have to have papers signed, says one of the girls, jiggling her bracelet at the orphans now doing jumping jacks to amuse them.

My mom bought one to go with my peach pants, says another girl. She sweats.

They watch the orphans paging through books, one even pokes at it as if it were electronic to show them she knows how to do tabs. One of them taps on the window with her head.

I wouldn't want that one doing my homework, says the front girl.

I have homework I really want done, says another girl.

The orphans behind the window show their labels: Chanel, Dior, Gap. Her dress doesn't even fit, says the last one about the last one.

Can you get one and just keep the clothes? asks the second girl who has backed away, bored.

I saw one that didn't have to have clothes, says the third, now the front. She wore a leash and looked like a lot of trouble.

A leash, repeated the second, in a voice as dreamy as the color of the marker the orphans inside smear across the window. With a leash, you never know who is really walking whom.

You'd like to think, says the front one.

They wander away. A spiky set of lights and a moving sidewalk lure them, the sidewalk coming right up next to them. But they're still into the shop. The front one accuses the last of orphanhood herself. You always count backward from ten before answering your mom, you talk nice when you don't have to.

The last one laughs. I count other things. It's you, because you accused me—you must be the orphan.

Orphan, orphan! the two un-accused girls scream, the sidewalk curling away.

The front one stomps the sidewalk still. Sighing, they all follow it back to the shop.

I wish they had thespians, or even lesbian orphans, says the third. My mom won't even allow me to buy their hankies—she's afraid I'll keep the bacteria.

We have to go home, says the front one, she mouths it to the watchers-in-the-window whereupon the orphans start throwing things. The orphans don't have much to throw, the clothes on themselves or in one case, a fake tooth that fell out earlier that makes a nice ping.

They think they're Christ on the cross, says the second girl. She sticks out her tongue.

An LCD starts across the bottom of the window, its readout only one: the statistic on how many orphans are made every minute. They put that on to make us feel sorry, says the front one.

I'll sympathy them with a half-hour of my mother, says the second girl. The orphans could always pretend to be dead.

Or be dead, says the third girl. Grateful is what they should be.

The three girls ditzy off but they don't leave it alone. I've got the one orphan's barcode, says the front one. I can look it up, see what she did.

I wouldn't bother, says the second girl. They'll spam. Anyway, she could have done something noble and not deserve it, or maybe she did nothing and somebody just dumped her. Sometimes the orphans are just sent back. Returns.

Who's got change? says the second girl.

The last girl turns out her purse and pockets for whatever's loose, the second one has a bill. The first is short but collects it all so it looks like she's not and runs back to the window with the money. The orphans go crazy, seeing the bills in her hand. They press on the bar beside the door but pellets drop from above. There's no way for the change to go in, the display is broken. Too bad.

The front girl puts her hand against an orphan's ear that's beside the glass. I'm getting into her head, she says. I'm telling her it isn't so bad.

They just think they're orphans, they have no proof—see that one who's writing down different names like she's choosing? says the second girl.

The other two watch the orphan press the paper against the glass. It's in some other language, says the second girl. None of them admit they can't read.

If I got one, my mom would kill me, says the last girl, turning away. She'd orphan us both or make me wear the orphan's clothes to school.

The second girl says, They don't have to go to school. How bad could it be?

The last girl comes back to watch with the other girls. One orphan pulls one of the others' mouths open, looking for another tooth to pull. Then they take turns pushing at the pellet bar until the floor is pelleted full.

I don't know, says the front one. Why don't they fight?

That's what we do, says the second girl.

Rats hate to fight, says the third one. We had a rat in class that jumped headfirst into the trash to avoid it.

The LCD counts backward.

The girls on both sides of the glass watch each other, the ones outside doing 3-2-1, the orphans slowly closing their eyes.

The lights go off in the orphan display.

The lights go up on three more orphans.

They can't all be orphans, yawns the last girl. Too many.

Oh? says the second girl. Watch.

The new orphans begin weeping, hands outstretched, they weep and look so sad in between. Finally, thespian orphans, says the second girl.

A long white sidewalk approaches them.

I had a dream I ended up an orphan, says the last girl. The parents popped off and didn't leave me anything. Imagine being that worthless.

The girls' eyes go blank while their brains imagine.

Roof-Topped

Our taxi driver produces a little tent from his trunk and carries it all the way up to the roof. It features a built-in mattress that we all try, one at a time. But first we splash off the day's dust under a bucket that waters the roof's geraniums, all five of us hot and nude and tar-footed, the summer stars sizzling and exploding about two minutes after we downed the last of the wine. Our taxi driver knows where to find the spigot and strips down first.

He also finds the roof and the pensione and the village, but that is partly our doing. Take us somewhere no one ever goes, we girls had commanded, only one day left in France. The taxi driver bowed to our gaggle of minis, the carnation taped to his jacket flopping. Why not? he'd agreed with an accent as sexy as how his black jeans hugged him, his curls touched his jacket, his t-shirt tightened across his chest, and his thick lips pronounced even *non* with resonance. You girls, he had said, you come with me. The village he chose lay in a crease marked in impossibly small print. As he flourished the map, the other drivers at the stand hooted. Did we deserve to set foot in this most perfect village of all of France, any of us? he demanded. *Oui, oui*, we cried, one louder than the other. Sternly, he demanded scissors. Marcy fished out the penknife she had hidden deep in her pack for keeping off rapists, and he cut the village right out of that crease.

Of course we insisted, and said we'd pay double to go. The mustache that hung over his lips quivered with *maybe*. A ride to the real France? He gave the finger to the other drivers as he squeezed the last girl inside his Citroen. Leaving town, we all sang "La Marseillaise" so badly a villager tossed a can down at us, and one of the Arab kids sleeping in a doorway shouted, *Te toit!* He drove us the long, long way, past any number of decent-sized roads, through villages so small nearly grown children waved at the car. Each of us took hour-long turns sitting beside his gear-shifting hand, each of us silently nauseous from being in the middle but so happy to be so close to that hand that did wander, yes, it did. The village, when we at last arrived, looked like any other. Granted, our judgment was somewhat impaired—it was dark by then and we had drunk most of a large jug of wine while killing an hour at the adjacent beach. Trailing sand, we staggered up the stairs to the rooftop.

A day later Marcy was the one who wouldn't leave the taxi for the plane. She was suffering from a severe sunburn from skinny dipping—*sans*, he kept telling her every time she took something off, sands, she said, yes, the lovely sand gets everywhere—and she said she couldn't bear sitting nine hours on the plane. She actually convinced the airline to reissue her ticket for medical reasons. The taxi driver—Jean-Philippe—said he had a mother who lived not far from the airport who would take her in for a few days.

The next time I saw her, Marcy was a puppeteer, part of a troupe encamped in my town park. Still single, I kept children in their seats in a public school setting, now on summer break. I was strolling behind the fountain, enjoying my freedom, when I recognized the stars her queen puppet was singing about, *So many and so pretty, roof-close and so itty-bitty*, and the map she rattled with a heart-shaped hole that led to nowhere. I asked Marcy about the map afterward. She was removing her son from his puppet costume that other pup-peteers "controlled" in postmodern whimsy. She said she had kept the cutout piece, that *Azpth* was how you pronounced the town, and that Jean-Philippe was really a circus fire-eater and drove a cab between jobs. Billings, she called them.

The other puppeteers blew smoke into the dark or shook hands with the lingering crowd. Her son whined for crackers she kept in a tin under the stage.

She hadn't believed the fire-eating bit either but they were soon enough without the cab and *à pied*, and after a few months of eating fire in various piazzas, he antagonized a fellow circus person who threw a cup of gasoline on him too early. She spent the rest of her pregnancy with Jean-Philippe covered in burns and confined to bed.

Funny, I stayed behind because of a burn too, she said.

Incroyable, I said.

We need some privacy now, she told her son who had eaten all the crackers and turned the tin upside down to bang on. Go amuse the others, she said. Go on. She collected the tin and his costume.

He thinks his father is Roquet, our carpenter, she said. Where was I? Since Jean-Philippe wouldn't take antibiotics because he wouldn't take charity and that's all we had, all I could do was weep into his wounds.

I'm sure all the salt cured him, I said.

It wasn't funny and she laughed too loudly, the way she had from behind her puppet screen. You are perhaps your old self, she said with her new-to-me French syntax. And Jean-Philippe did have a mother, she said. But not living so near the airport.

I offered her a Gauloise I still smoked in honor of our trip. The irony was, she said, pocketing the cigarette, that he died of a drug overdose a year later. Drugs! No antibiotics for him, *petit chou*.

He was violent, she said. On those drugs.

A crowd was applauding her son. He was doing a sort of Russian squat dance on top of the ticket taker's table. At his age—four, five?—there was no hiding the wildness.

She turned away to sort the wooden legs of a limp king. Puppets were perfect for me, she went on. No one could see how pregnant I was behind the curtain. Once I even nursed and pulled the strings. Now that's real acrobatics.

She made the king bow.

We weren't much good at anything then, I said.

I don't know, she said, watching me watch the king dance. He did all of us that night—didn't he?

I had been so sophisticated, plugging my ears with the others, standing in the stairwell smoking, waiting for my turn, waiting for Marcy to come down off the roof. Maybe I was sophisticated then and it's now that I'm not. Next, *tout de suite*, he'd yelled.

He could have made any of us pregnant, she said. Solemn and sisterly, she gave me a kiss on both my cheeks and turned back to her packing of props.

The king lay on his back, his gaze caught in some crack of the dark sky she left him under.

For me, he was still a French cabbie, a *roué* who commandeered our trip, stopped at a hotel that would let us sleep on the roof, unfolded a pup tent from his trunk, the man who had found me sacred, inviolable.

She had merely been clever about missing her flight.

I applauded the child she had produced, the puppets who never would get it right. I had my own version.

In Black and White

Henry does not want to sink heel or toe into it. He unlaces and removes his nice shoes and then parts the cane and thorn and rubbish that the land here offers over itself but the laces snag even in his uplifted hand, and the thorns scrape deep into its white side. What I hear is what you might, words he learned from his mammy, or so he says his father calls her when she curses, words I can hear even over the pump and the new child, even over the gush of one and the howl of the other. As Henry fights his way through the briars in his socks, curses his way past the Cad and the boat and the Something Else vehicle you can't see from the street, the thorns are so thick, the rat-pink baby limbs get soap-rinsed and so slippery some tight gripping is involved, then some quick wrapping and baby soothing, some milk up front.

He kisses us both, all lips buss air, and he pinches my cheek bottom to make the baby suck harder.

He is putting in the horse stove, I say. Inside.

Henry says he has such a movie he is going to make, he is almost sure to make. Where is this stove?

Before I can think how he has to steer past the fallen wood and shingles to the stove place, the baby, nakedly post-pumpbath nursing, pees straight up at me, pees right into my ear as my head is turned toward Henry who now finds a smile you could shake up and find frothy.

He spots the horse stove through the uprights, he waves as I work the towel, he heads in.

The horse stove sits upright but is not yet chimneyed. So covered in soot—secondhand soot because the stove had a life in another house where its horse-embossed front glowed so orange in its heating that we made an offer on the spot—he throws off a black cloud when he and Henry tender their handshakes, while the boards he has taken out or down shift under their effort, and some even threaten to fall. Henry waves at them too, without touching them. They teeter, they fall back the way they should.

He says he's brought beer and hors d'oeuvres and news about his movie and what about dinner?

Henry gets backpatted out through the doorless kitchen and into the backyard where tree limbs hang and the thorns all around have been almost all held back with thick silver tape so you can sit in amongst them. I expect I'll find another seat soon, says the father of this baby as he bends down to adjust three bucket seats all entwined in vine. The thorns gave up half a gas pump last time we weed-whacked.

Together they dig a pit beside the three seats and somehow Henry's pressed-sharp pants don't get dirty even though he puts coals down its sides in a basket fashion, layer on layer, while the father of the baby gathers sticks out of the thorns and then they light it, with the wood of the matches they ruin.

Henry's girl shows, out of the blue. She's the salt to his pepper, she's trouble and fun, invited, of course, but unexpected. Her taxi comes from the train while I'm wrestling the not quite sleeping baby into the suitcase that holds his blankets and diapers and, with it left open, just barely him. I leave it close to the hotdogs, the spare ones for breakfast, so the dog will watch him. Then I go join Henry's girl where she is fitting herself into the last seat, I go to squat by the fire and laugh.

The bugs sure hate the fire, Henry says into the dusk that settles in as fast as the smoke. This is what we all say after the wieners are roasted and the last of the chips—Henry's hors d'oeuvres—are taken care of by the dog who knows a chip in a bush is better than wrapped breakfast dogs beside a baby, this is what we say while we swat and laugh. Then we bless that fire with beer sprinklings and, surprise, the bugs change over its steam into stars, snapping other stars at a distance.

Stars of another kind are what the men talk of, who's got what tune and via what talent or video. Henry's girl and I ask how much of this talk will have to be talked up to beard the long night. We have heard about talent before, about their agents and backups and deals and schedules. I swing the baby, trying to wake, on a branch, I swing him to a little tune about stars the others barely remember.

You like this place? asks Henry.

We haven't found any bodies yet, the father of the baby says and chocks one up. Though it does smell a little.

It's sewage, I say like that's a comfort. At least we have the pump.

I could never buy here, he says, I can't wear Ferragamos or the cops here will think they're hot. With Guccis they figure I can pay them off, I've got to have real money, not credit. He shines his left shoe with a leaf. It's a beach like the Hamptons or nothing.

What water we have is not so far away, and water—the chugging of a washer, the sink spigot—is all that will calm the baby who now needs it. Without a washer or a sink, we must walk down the dark chunked-up asphalt road, between reeds, cattails and the bedsprings that lie strewn along it, walk to the back porch of a neighbor, or, rather, an ex-neighbor who lives now in some less sheriff x-ed out place, then walk up to our knees into the water that drifts over his back porch. The baby's little legs thrash and then dangle from the railing under which armored crabs swim, chained one to the other in an ecstasy of summer and crab sex, a five- or ten-crab chain that weaves around our ankles under a flashlight Henry holds.

It's perfect, he says. How much for the location?

We laugh. Stars wouldn't come here, I say. They would have to be borne here on sedan chairs.

They would have to be born here, says Henry's girl. But who comes from here who would want to come back?

She only pretends no interest in stars, she has their numbers. You can almost hear her packaging them, the ribbons coming together, the six or seven figures. She's Henry's one-way to the Hamptons.

They wouldn't have to stay the night, I say. You don't either.

But I've brought the sleeping bags you suggested, she says. And coffee so they could work.

The baby, carried all this way by his father, signals his opinion of work. The baby really loves the movies, says his father over his crying, he will keep his eyes open for as long as it takes.

We're in his movie, I say. It's a classic.

Henry takes the little guy bare chest to bare chest, and offers his heart to him until he's quiet. There's so much silence we can hear the two pumps, the crabs underwater, the bugs in the reeds scraping their bellies, and the tide at the sand.

The moon rises.

Camera, action, says the baby's father.

ACKNOWLEDGMENTS

AGNI: "Swordfish in Nantucket"

Bennington Review: "Burn the Bed"

Bomb: "Roof-Topped"

Brooklyn Rail: "London Boy," "Read the Snow," "The Stroke of Midnight"

Conjunctions: "Don't Look Now," "Loose Lion"

December: "Silent Night"

Epiphany: "The Red and Purple Blooms"

Evergreen Review: "Knife Block"

Exacting Clam: "Motherliness"

Exterminating Angel: "The Oscars"

Failbetter: "Swanbit"

14 Hills: "The Movie Business"

Freight Stories: "Christ and Three Geese and What Happened to the Boy Afterward"

Great Jones Street: "80s Lilies," "Niagara"

Guernica: "Frangipani"

Indiana Review: "80s Lilies"

Joyland: "Man Is Born to Trouble as the Sparks Fly Upward"

Kenyon Review: "The Cloud Painter's Lover"

Lit: "Decorum Stinks"

Literarian: "Kosciuszko Bridge," "Mexican Honeymoon"

Literary Review: "The Haight"

Litro: "White Supremacist"

Matchbook: "Orphan Shop"
Mississippi Review: "Weatherproof"
Moonshot: "The Long Swim" (as "Branded")
Narrative: "Mr. Schmeckler"
New World Writing: "Niagara," "We Are Learning How to Talk"
O. Henry Prize Collection Series: "80s Lilies"
Opium: "Rex Rhymes with It"
Strange Attractors: "Fortuneteller"
Tin House: "The Last Night"
Vol. 1 Brooklyn: "Camp beside Water" (as "Camp Talk")
West Branch Wired: "Ottawa"
Wigleaf: "Horses on My Side"
Witness: "Two Dog High"
Yale Review: "In Black and White"

"Read the Snow" and "Roof-Topped" received Pushcart Prize special mentions.

Thank you so much to Steve Bull, Julia Ringo, Gay Waley, Molly Giles, Katherine Arnoldi, Roberta Allen, Dawn Raffel, the Lochridges whom I love dearly, JoAnn Hanley, Tim Purtell, Betsy Newman, the Corporation of Yaddo, MacDowell, the Hawthornden Castle Writers Retreat, Rowlands Writers Retreat, Headlands Center for the Arts, James Merrill House, Bogliasco Foundation, the Guggenheim Foundation, and the New York Foundation for the Arts. I would also like to express my appreciation for the work of all the editors who published the stories, the deft crew at the press who made this collection happen, and most especially Robin McLean who chose it.

JUNIPER
JUNIPER PRIZE FOR FICTION

This volume is the twenty-seventh recipient
of the Juniper Prize for Fiction,
established in 2004 by the
University of Massachusetts Press
in collaboration with the
UMass Amherst MFA Program
for Poets and Writers, to be
presented annually for an outstanding
work of literary fiction. Like its sister award,
the Juniper Prize for Poetry established
in 1976, the prize is named in honor
of Robert Francis (1901–1987),
who lived for many years at
Fort Juniper, Amherst, Massachusetts.